LOVE AND
OTHER WOUNDS

ecco
An Imprint of HarperCollins*Publishers*

LOVE
AND
OTHER WOUNDS

STORIES

JORDAN HARPER

LOVE AND OTHER WOUNDS. Copyright © 2015 by Jordan Harper. All rights reserved. Printed in the United States of America. No part of this book may be used or reproduced in any manner whatsoever without written permission except in the case of brief quotations embodied in critical articles and reviews. For information address HarperCollins Publishers, 195 Broadway, New York, NY 10007.

HarperCollins books may be purchased for educational, business, or sales promotional use. For information please e-mail the Special Markets Department at SPsales@harpercollins.com.

FIRST EDITION

Designed by Suet Yee Chong
Title page photograph by Suet Yee Chong
Cover photograph © by Nancy Newberry

Library of Congress Cataloging-in-Publication Data has been applied for.

ISBN 978-0-06-239438-5

15 16 17 18 19   OV/RRD   10 9 8 7 6 5 4 3 2 1

For David and Sheryl Harper

CONTENTS

LOVE AND OTHER WOUNDS

AGUA DULCE

John ran through the high desert, away from his grave. He followed the power lines through scrub-covered hills. The power lines hummed. They whispered things he couldn't understand. But that was just madness leaking from his triple-fucked brain. Just like the sparkles and flashes at the corners of his vision and the way his head throbbed in time with his heart, frantic. The pulse radiated from his scalp where Carter had taken the pistol to him.

John's mouth felt full of hot pennies. He spat a mouthful of blood. Some splashed on the brush and pebbles underfoot. Some dribbled down onto his jeans. John wiped red drool off his chin. His hands were caked in desert dirt from the grave Carter had made him dig. Jesus, his head. Triple-fucked indeed. Brain-swamped from death-fear shakes and meth hunger.

Skull-rattled from the pistol-whipping. Whole-body blasted from the orange pills Carter had fed him.

John raced tumbleweeds and thought of death. Back in the desert, as he dug his own grave, death had come so close John could still feel ghost maggots crawling under his skin. And death could still be coming. Carter could be running behind him. It would take more than a shovel swung by a crank-skinny suckmouth like John to lay out Carter. Carter could be tracking him by torn earth and trampled scrub and spat blood. Carter could be aiming at his back right now, ready to send a bullet through John's brain and end this whole stupid mess. Lord, nothingness sounded so sweet. John didn't know why he ran from it.

John couldn't do much, but he could run. He was made of rope and bone. Meth had melted the rest. He could run all day, even in the fire-season oven of the California high desert.

After he'd hit Carter with the shovel, the power lines were the first things he'd seen. So he followed them. If he'd chosen right, the power lines would lead him out of the high desert and back to Agua Dulce. Down in Agua Dulce, in a motel room looking out at rock and rattlesnake warning signs, the boy sat on the bed, probably eating a vending machine supper of soda and pork rinds. Watching teevee.

The power lines led him into a canyon between two high-backed hills. He moved into the shade of the valley. Underfoot the scrub was so dry it begged to burn, like ill will alone might ignite it. As he entered the wind tunnel of the valley, John smelled cow shit.

The longhorn ranch. When Carter had driven him up the mountain, John making the trip wrapped up in the bed of Carter's truck, he'd caught this same whiff of cow dung. On the other side of the cattle ranch would be the road. They'd been moving uphill then, so he could take the downhill path back to Agua Dulce and . . .

Gunshot.

John's body reacted to the sound before the noise hit his brain. He froze. Pissed a trickle. Knew:

Carter was coming.

Late at night when the meth burned itself down to a dim glow at the back of his eyes, his teeth grinding so hard he could taste enamel dust, John knew plenty well that no one with a whole mind and a healthy disposition would owe as much money and crank credit to the High Desert chapter of Aryan Steel as he did. Aryan Steel, lockdown-born and baptized in shank-drawn blood, was made up of mad crackers too crazy for the businessmen who ran the Aryan Brotherhood. Aryan Steel's name carried heavy weight among badass rednecks west of the Mississippi. In Broken Arrow, in the Huntsville yard, in Little Rock, in Big Tuna, folks knew to step careful when they saw a man with a blue lightning bolt or two tattooed on his arm. A blue bolt tat meant the wearer had killed on an Aryan Steel greenlight.

Carter had two blue bolts on his arm the day John met him at the Shady Lady in Fontana. John had been a Hells Angels prospect once, and he had a name with some weight of its own. That was before the crank and booze and everything else. Now he was just a suckmouth with brown teeth and slippery eyes. John bought cheap Mexi crystal from Carter, the kind that dripped down the back of the throat like slow napalm for hours. John took credit when it was offered, then begged for it to be extended. But maybe John knew the whole time in the back of his brain, where the rot was blackest, that he wasn't buying meth from Carter. He was putting down payments on a slow-motion suicide.

The bill came due that morning in a shitty motel room in

Agua Dulce. John had muled a couple pounds of coke for the Steel to chip a couple hundred off his tab. The pounds were on the coffee table. Carter was going to meet him at the room, pick up the pounds, and trade him a teenth of crystal.

Three blue thunderbolt tattoos rode on Carter's bicep. John wasn't sure when the third one had shown up. It seemed like a thing a man ought to have noticed. Carter bagged the three pounds in a backpack while shooting eyes at the boy.

"The fuck is that?" Carter asked as he pushed a bindle across the table.

"That's my boy."

Carter shook his head as he packed up the pounds John had brought.

"You're shitting me. You brought a kid."

"His bitch mom left him with me for the weekend. She's off down to Primm Valley."

Carter laughed. Primm Valley was the first place to gamble over the Nevada line. The bitch told folks she didn't like Vegas. She said she didn't care about neon lights and faggots riding tigers. But the truth was—and John knew Carter could guess—she couldn't wait the extra forty miles to Vegas. The boy's mother had the casino jones. With a degenerate gambler mom and a suckmouth dad, the boy was doomed to grow up thirsty for something. Only question was what.

Carter walked over to the window. Outside, Agua Dulce baked. The back of the motel faced a barbed-wire fence plastered in yellow rattlesnake warning signs. Carter turned back around. There were pills in Carter's palm. The pills were orange-soda orange.

"Take them," Carter said.

"Man, I can't get down like that." John nodded toward the boy.

"Don't remember asking," Carter said.

John took the orange pills in his palm. He tried to ID them.

"Didn't give them to you to read, motherfucker. Take them."

John put them in his mouth. That same old pill-bitter slime coated his mouth. The taste brought memories of a hundred memoryless days. He looked over at the boy watching teevee. Something with wings was stuck in John's chest. The wings beat against his rib cage. He swallowed the pills dry.

"Somebody else know where this kid is?" Carter asked.

"Why?"

"You know why."

And there it was. John wrote down the bitch's cell phone number and tucked it in the boy's pocket. He thought about kissing the boy on the top of the head, but he didn't know how.

"Boy. Going to step out. You wait for your momma here and buy something out the snack machine if you get hungry."

Two pickup trucks sat parked outside the room. One John recognized as Carter's. The other one, a rusted-out old Ram, had three Aryan Steel cowboys standing around it in wifebeaters and face tattoos. John counted five blue bolts between them. Behind the wheel was a fresh-faced recruit, his scalp still fishbelly white. The recruit, nineteen tops, had only one piece of ink, a still-wet Iron Cross. He looked scared, as if he were the one about to take his last ride.

The orange pills kicked in. Or maybe it was something else. John sank to the pavement as the world panned and zoomed. Blue-bolt-marked arms lifted him off the pavement, carried him to the back of the truck. He climbed into the truck bed on his own power. They wrapped him in a section of chain link and half-covered him with a mildewed tarp. Carter tossed a shovel next to him and told the others he'd go it alone. He flexed his bicep. Three blue bolts swelled.

"Room for number four," Carter said with a smile. He covered John's face with the tarp.

The drive into the desert passed in an orange-pill haze. The truck climbed. John sweated himself into jerky. He closed his eyes and saw the boy, wished he could see anything else. Finally the truck stopped and Carter pulled off the tarp. John's eyes solarized. Nothing but high desert scrub and power lines far off. Carter handed John the shovel and gestured to a patch of desert.

"Dig." Carter scratched himself under the chin with his big-ass pistol.

John dug. The dry soil was hard going at first as John sketched out a hole about his own size. Maybe it was the pills or the dumb animal shock, but he dug without contemplating the crawl into it, the pistol blast, and the eternity that would follow it.

"Good enough," Carter said. "Stand in it."

And something ancient and not yet dead came out of John's lizard brain like a solid thing, swallowing up his chest and holding it tight. Carter saw him hesitate and swung the pistol butt into John's skull. John went down in the dirt. He saw the shovel and he thought of the boy and the shovel swung and Carter was on the ground. John missed his moment to finish him. John ran into the desert instead.

John moved down the valley toward the smell of cow shit. The longhorns were sealed off from the valley by a barbed-wire fence. Carter winged a few more shots at him. None close. Bullets bounced off rocks. And then there was a popping noise and a power line clipped by a ricochet snapped and fell, spitting sparks into the desert scrub below.

John moved toward the barbed-wire fence. He smelled

smoke. He risked a look behind him. The power line twisted around in the scrub like a beheaded rattlesnake. It puked sparks. Fire and smoke sprung up faster than John could believe.

Wildfire.

Any boy raised up in the California high desert knew to fear smoke and fire. It was how a chemical-laced suckmouth like John managed to avoid smoking. Every match tossed aside, each careless cigarette butt could set one off. Miles of burned brush, acres of black smoke. When the wind blew dry and sure—like it did today—a wildfire could gobble up a hillside faster than a man could run.

Running was the smart thing to do. The fire gave John a chance. If he could make it through the cattle pen fast enough he'd make it to the road on the other side before Carter could catch up. He saw a metal shack on the other side of the gravel road. His brain begged him to hide. But this was no time for going to ground. John wanted to run.

John reached the fence. A longhorn bull stood on the other side. The steer stared straight ahead. His horns hung over the fence. John grabbed them. The steer didn't move. John put a foot on the bottom strand of barbed wire. It wobbled under his weight.

John put his foot on the second strand. All his weight was on the steer when the gunshot came. Blood and meat and hide exploded from the bull's shoulder. The bull roared. It tossed its head. Barbed wire ripped John's legs from thigh to knee as the bull tossed him into the pen. The ground slapped the air out of him. He gasped uselessly for agonizing seconds, trying to remember how to breathe. He dodged hooves as he rolled. He took a bath in cow shit. The animals, already spooked by the smoke drifting in from the valley, scrambled across their pen as bullets tore into them. John made it to his feet and looked behind him. Carter had made it to the high side of the hill faster than John had figured was possible. But he had no way to reach John.

John made it to the gate that connected the pen to the road. Metal slats were easier to hop than barbed wire. Blood spots soaked John's jeans. Blood squirted between his teeth. Dark-lights strobed in his eyes. His smoke-lashed lungs were bundles of raw nerves. But he was not dead yet. His feet touched the gravel road and he felt home free. The road down would lead to Agua Dulce and the—

Well, fuck.

A rusted-out Ram climbed the road. Devil dust swarmed around it, spiraled up in eddies toward the cloudless sky. The men in the back of the truck had shaved heads. They had tat-toos on their faces and necks. They had hunting rifles. They barked out rebel yells. Aryan Steel. Carter's cavalry. Carter's cell phone must have caught a rare signal in the desert.

Plumes of smoke hugged the earth. A thick black cloud laid itself between the truck and John. The truck paused downhill of the cattle pen to stay in the breathable air. John looked up the hill. The fire cut off that line of retreat. Jesus, it had spread fast. Too fast. The open desert was in flames. He turned back to the truck. Rifles trained on him. The standoff had a shelf life. The fire was climbing into the cattle pen. Soon it would surround them.

Then the skinheads looked to their right, toward the metal shack. A rancher stood in its doorway. He had a shotgun trained on the truck. He had the Aryan Steel killers cold. He said some-thing to them, quiet. They lowered their rifles. They knew a desert rancher would fire on armed trespassers. They knew what a tight spread of buckshot could do to them. Relief soaked John, numbed his pain.

Gunshot.

The rancher's jaw sheared off. He dropped his shotgun. His hands grasped at bloody air where his chin had been. Carter came out of the smoke below the cattle pen and fired again. The other skinheads trained their rifles on the rancher and opened up on him. He jitterbugged into death. Carter looked up the road and locked eyes with John. His face was a red mask from the shovel wound on his scalp. His teeth were bright white as he smiled at his prey.

A longhorn screamed in pain and fear. The fire had spread to the hay in the pen. The cattle swirled in the pen, running from smoke and sparks.

"Come. To. Us. Or."

Carter had climbed onto the hood of the truck. He shouted out the terms of John's surrender over the screams of the terrified longhorns. Carter yelled one word at a time.

"I," Carter said.

"Will," Carter said.

"Kill," Carter said.

"The," Carter said.

"Boy," Carter said.

John stopped. It wasn't a bluff. A little while back an Aryan Steel roughneck had shotgunned a six-year-old just for having the dumb luck to be at a "leave no witnesses" greenlight in Texas. There was no chance John would make it back to Agua Dulce ahead of the truck. Carter would kill the boy just to teach other suckmouths not to run.

So die and get it over with, John thought. There hadn't been a reason to run from the grave in the first place other than his body's own cussed foolish affection for its own existence. It had been a bad call, and the cost was a dead rancher and a wildfire and cattle burning. So die. The boy might have one bad day of nothing but sink water and pork rinds before his bitch mom gets back from Primm Valley. And then the boy would have a whole life of no shitheel dad, no prison visiting rooms, no MoonPie birthday cakes and gas-station-bought birthday presents. Today could wind up to be the best day in the boy's life, and he just didn't know it yet. Do the boy a favor and die.

He walked toward them with his hands raised in the air. Smoke swirled, sending the world in and out of existence. Aryan Steel sent the recruit out to meet him, a pistol in the kid's hand. John would be his first blue bolt. Why not? John passed the gate of the cattle yard. Now the yard was burning something fierce. He saw a longhorn pressing itself into the fence, not caring about the way the barbs tore at its flesh. Its eyes begged John. It hit John in the lizard brain. It vibrated in his nerves and the sockets of his teeth.

Out of the smoke a flaming piece of tumbleweed like a comet collided with John. He hit the gravel as the bush rolled over him. He saw the boy sitting alone in the hotel room. The bush rolled back into the smoke. John felt his shirt burning. He tore it off as he stood. Another wave of smoke hit him, and as the smoke coated his throat he saw the boy again and then the smoke cleared and he saw the gate. And he saw a way maybe to save the boy and maybe even himself too.

He ran to the gate. The skinhead recruit watched him dumbly. A metal drop bar held the gate shut. John yanked at it. Longhorns dug into each other. John looked behind him. Carter had figured it out and was yelling at the recruit. The recruit had the keys to the truck. The others were stuck without him. A curtain of smoke drew itself shut between Carter and John.

John opened the gate. The cattle stampeded. The recruit

went down fast. A horn tore his arm up. The pistol hit the gravel. The boy reached down after it. A hoof dented his head. His eyes popped out. The cattle headed down into the smoke. John moved to follow. He passed the dead rancher and scooped up his shotgun. Then the smoke got John. It hit him, got inside him. His eyes burned, his nose, the insides of his ears. Pain everywhere. He dropped to his knees. He crawled through hot gravel. He could hear cattle screams and gunfire and men begging Jesus and their mothers. He came out the other side into horror and hell.

A longhorn bull engulfed in flames galloped uphill, back toward the truck. It trampled a dead skinhead. A man with a face tattoo fired twice into the animal's skull before it hit him. When the bull fell, the ground shook underfoot. The man fell underneath it, burning, crushed. His broken chest rattled above the hiss of the fire. John came up to him and stove his head in with the butt of the twelve-gauge. Every shell counted.

The fire was on them now. The air was thick with heat. The oxygen was eaten clean out of it. John couldn't catch his breath. A fire devil like a cone of flame danced across the road. The truck caught fire. Its tires exploded in four quick bursts. A shirtless Nazi, a beard of blood pouring from his broken front teeth, had taken shelter in the cab of the truck. He screamed as the upholstery melted onto his skin. He scrambled for the door handle. He fell onto the gravel, rolled trying to put the fire out. The upholstery sizzled into him as John walked by with the shotgun raised.

Carter came up from the truck bed. He was bleeding from a bad chest gash. His big-ass pistol barked. The bullet took John high in the chest, a through-and-through wound. It burned. Now John was cooking on the inside too. Blood bubbled in pink foam from the entrance wound. John knew that meant a lung shot. He was dying. For the first time in a long time, he didn't want to die.

Carter fumbled for a reload. Bullets dripped through bloody fingers. They bounced on the gravel. Carter raised the unloaded pistol. John stared down the barrel at nothing. Carter dry-fired an empty gun. He said something John would never know. He smiled as John put the shotgun to his head. The buckshot made Carter's head go away.

John walked down the road. The fire sang and sang. Helicopters flew overhead, covered in cop emblems and news team logos. The animals of the high desert moved with John down the road, down the mountain. A coyote ran past him. Rattlesnakes slithered down the road, ignoring the mice and lizards that ran with it. No predators or prey anymore. John moved slowly. He saw things that might have been Gila monsters or just flashes of smoke madness. He trudged as if the pebbles at his feet were snowbanks. He hunched over himself, too weak to lift his head off his blood-bubbling chest. He knew he wasn't going to make it.

A longhorn with burnt flesh pink like a baby's skin trotted out of the smoke. Sparks shook off its hooves. John grabbed a horn. He slumped over its back. He rode the steer down, down. He would never be sure what happened on that ride, what was real and what was smoke dreams. At the bottom of the mountain he came out of the smoke on the back of the bull like something out of a Greek myth, like a man who went down to hell to fetch not his bride but himself.

Around him, the animals of the mountain fled from the fire into the streets of Agua Dulce. They swarmed among the fire trucks and cop cars. People filmed them with their phones. John clung to the bull as it clopped down a store-lined street. Finally a fireman spotted John and pulled him off the steer's back.

"Johnny," John said through fire-cracked lips as someone strapped a plastic mask over his mouth. The mask blasted him off to pure-oxygen heaven.

"Somebody go fetch Johnny," he said. "Somebody go fetch my boy."

PROVE IT ALL NIGHT

No future, no past.

Just that animal now. All the fears and doubts and memories are gone and there's nothing left but me and the single moment that flows around me.

I don't find peace in some ashram or on a therapist's couch. It's here in this gun and this car, and through that glass door. It's inside the gas station as I burst through the door. It's pouring like tears from the terrified eyes of the clerk. It's inside that cash register. It's under the counter as the scared man's hands go out of view. It's in that moment when maybe it's money he's going for or maybe it's a shotgun to silly string my guts on the chip rack behind me. I tell you that moment lasts forever and blinks by like it's nothing.

It's money. He fills a plastic bag with shaking hands.

My ears fill with blood so that the Muzak turns itself down and all I can hear is my heartbeat and the click of the hammer as I thumb it back to show the man I mean business. I hear the jagged hiss of his breath and he's right here in the moment with me. He's not thinking of next month's rent or the way he thought life would be when he was back in high school. No. He is here with me, and only me. I tell him to throw in a carton of Camel Wides.

In front of the gas station comes a honk, Mark telling me the clock is running. Time is still passing after all, the honk says, so move along little lady. I scoop up the cash and the cartons of Camels and I run to the car. Mark's got the passenger side door waiting open for me and I slide in and the back tires spit gravel until they sink their teeth into the asphalt beneath and we rocket out onto the road.

Mark likes that loud deep heavy metal as his getaway music so that's what pours through the speakers as we head down the road. The wind whips his hair—it grows like the rain forest, and I can't keep my hands out of it—and that devil's smile splits his face and I know now how he looks so animal and alive. He's found the magic elixir: armed robbery.

I crash back into myself like one of those old-timey trick divers who'd jump off a roof into a kiddie pool. Time isn't timeless anymore, the world isn't infinite. It's 1994 and we're someplace in the middle of Missouri, on some curvy old road that used to be Route 66.

"How'd we do?" he asks me.

I show him fistfuls of money and dump the carton of smokes in the backseat. There's four other cartons back there already. They're sort of like the scalps we've been taking all night. But that fifth one was the first one for me, the first one with the gun in my hands instead of his.

"Oh my god," I say. I can feel the strings of my flesh all individual rubbing against each other inside me.

"I toldja," he says.

"I want to do another one," I say.

My mom pierced my ears when I was four years old. She took an ice cube from the freezer and cracked it in two with her molar. She made a sandwich of them with my left lobe as the meat. She held the ice there until the lobe froze into numbness and a dull ache. Then she took a sewing needle in her right hand and the heel of a potato in the other. She held the potato behind my ear. She pushed the needle through my frozen lobe and into the potato backstop. And I screamed as the needle found the center of the lobe where the nerves weren't dead and pain pushed through the cold.

The day I meet Mark I am seventeen and just as full of nothing but cold ache and numbness. And Mark—twenty-one and on parole, with a car bought on credit from a stupid man—is the needle through the heart of me.

"Where are you going?" he asks me.

"You tell me," I say.

And he smiles. Sometimes it really is that easy.

We drive for days. We drive across the state. We eat road burgers and sausage biscuits. We fuck in the front seat and sleep in the back. We buy cassettes in small-town record stores and gas stations. We listen to doo-wop, gangsta rap, drug-fueled weirdness. We crank it all up loud. We blow the speakers three days in. We blow all our money in four.

Mark won't let me fret. He points out people driving next to us. He tells me that most of them—most everybody—is screaming almost all of the time.

"They're just screaming real quiet," he says. "It's true, you know. Look around at the faces on the bus. Look at the guy taking your order and pushing the plastic tray, the plastic-wrapped burger with plastic cheese, look at the face he's wearing under the smile. You listen and tell me he's not screaming.

"It's part of the human condition," Mark says. "Humans went and built their own cages, and they didn't fucking build a door. We are the result of unnaturalness. You ever see a dog chew up his own leg? I mean chew it until it bled, just out of plain worry?"

I nod.

"No animal out in the wild ever chewed its own leg into hamburger for no reason. No, it's only cages, real or in the mind, that make an animal chew at itself."

He takes my hand in his—the touch causes my heart to double-time—and turns it so I can see my own fingers. The nail tips arc out just over the tips of my fingers. They aren't chewed ragged the way I'd kept them since I was ten years old.

"You stopped chewing at your leg. You feeling free?"

I answer without words. My hand in the crotch of his jeans finds him half hard already. I feel his devil's smile on my own face as I fish his cock out into the night air.

"Drive straight," I say. "Drive slow. You crash into something or slam on the brakes, I won't be responsible for my reactions." I click my teeth so he gets the picture. And then I swallow him all the way down. He drives straight, but not slow. The wind whips and roars around us as he pushes his foot down on the gas and his hand down on my head. I can feel what I'm doing to him in the throbbing hardness in my mouth and the jerks of his stomach muscles. As his hips buck and he shoots down my throat I realize both his hands hold my head, not the wheel, and the car roars pilotless down the road as I drink him in.

We start our spree an hour later.

One two three four five gas stations and liquor stores before 4 A.M.

After I take down my first one, I want one more. He thinks it over, nods. "One more and we steer the ship to Florida," he said. "I heard the coffee in Miami is stronger than the coke. I say let's have them both and give it the old Pepsi challenge."

We find a gas station that meets our needs. Close to a highway junction, empty of customers, in good enough repair to suggest the robbery will be worth our time. We park in front of it, a few spots down from the door so the clerk won't be able to see our car.

"Can I go again?" I ask him, taking the revolver from the glove box.

"Fortune favors the bold," he says back. Then he steals a kiss and the pistol from my hand. "But you're not yet bold enough."

He yanks the ski mask down. He heads into the gas station and I shift over to the driver's seat just as the cop car pulls in next to me. The world turns down the volume again. There's two of them. The cop sitting shotgun gets out carrying a plastic mug with a logo of the gas station on it, like he always comes here for refills. My hand inches up to the horn, to give two short blasts like we planned, to let Mark know to come out shooting.

But I don't do it.

My hand drifts over to the gearshift and I put the car in reverse. That's about the moment Mark comes out the door of the gas station with a bag full of cash in one hand and the pistol in the other. He sees the cop and the cop sees him and the plastic cup drops out of view as the cop goes for his gun and Mark pulls the trigger and then the cop drops from sight as well. The other cop dumps out the door and takes cover behind his car and draws down. And Mark looks to me for a split second and his eyes say everything: Put it in drive. Slam on the gas. Smoosh this motherfucker like the mosquito he is. And we'll ride this moment on out till it ends, and maybe we'll die but we'll live every moment until we do. And I understand it all in that split second.

But I don't do it.

I turn the wheel the other way. I pull out toward the highway. I can still see his eyes in the rearview as the cop comes up shooting and Mark fires back, five times, putting that cop down on the gravel. When I read about it in the papers later, the coroner says said Mark must have pulled the trigger those last few times on some animal instinct, cause the cop's first and only shot went through Mark's skull and cleaned his brainpan straight out.

I drive and drive and although once I hear sirens that make me freeze like a rabbit in the desert they fade away after a while and I keep driving. I leave the car up in North St. Louis with the keys sitting on the driver's seat. I leave everything but enough money to get me home.

After that there's not much to tell you. My life has gone the way it was supposed to go. I work in an office. I married a good enough man with a job and scared eyes and we never went bust and we never went boom. Yesterday I watched my mother, hollowed out, with tubes jammed in her and thousand-dollar pills that could keep her on just this side of the shadow for another week, and on the ride home my husband and I held hands and I told him don't you ever let that be me. And he lied to me and told me he wouldn't and I lied to him and told him the same.

Sometimes I hear Mark laugh, and some days in the car the right song will come on the satellite radio and I'll feel him there tingling like a phantom limb. Like he's sitting there next to me in the dark. But I know that's not so. And I know that when you die there's not even darkness, and I know Mark and me won't meet on some cloud or in some pit of fire. And I guess that's a good thing. I couldn't take those eyes seeing what's become of me, those eyes looking down at my hands and my chewed-up ragged nails.

LUCY IN THE PIT

If she pisses, she lives.

Lucy's gums are bone white, whiter than the teeth set into them. It is a sign of shock. Her body is shutting down, one system at a time. Kidneys close shop first. If she pisses, it means her body is starting up again. If she doesn't, her blood will fill with poisons and she will die.

If Lucy was my dog I would not have matched her against Tuna. Four pounds is a serious advantage for a sixty-pound dog. It should have been a forfeit. But Jesse needed the money. I told myself that I let him get his way because he is Lucy's owner and I am just her handler.

Icy wind off Lake Erie rocks the truck, making me swerve. I pull my hand back from Lucy's mouth and put it back on the wheel. I must drive steady. I must not speed. I cannot risk the police pulling us over. Lucy would die on the side of the road while I sat helpless in handcuffs.

Lucy's fur is the color of a bad day. Deep gray turned to black where the blood soaks her. Her blood is everywhere. There is gauze over a bad bleeder on the thick muscles of her neck where Tuna savaged her. I wanted to end the fight then, pick Lucy up and declare Tuna the victor. But Jesse said no. Again I let him win. And Lucy scratched the floor trying to get back in the fight.

Tough little bitch. Proud little warrior.

She cannot fight again. Her front leg will never be the same. After tonight she can retire, she can breed, she can heal. But she isn't done yet. We both have a fight waiting for us in the hotel room.

I am a dogman. I breed fighting dogs. I train fighting dogs to fight better. I take fighting dogs to their fights and I handle them in the pit. This is what I do. It may not be your way but it is an old way. My father was a dogman. He learned the trade from my grandfather, and he taught it to me. I have seen dogs fight and bleed and die. I have cheered them on as they fought. It can be cruel.

There are dogfighters who beat their dogs, who whip them and starve them thinking to make the dogs savage. There's those who kill their curs, who drown them or shock them and then burn their bodies in the backyard. Some men fight their dogs to the death every time, no quarter asked for or given. Some men fight their dogs in garbage-strewn alleys with rats watching on greedily, the rats knowing they'll get to feed on the corpse of the loser.

There is another way. In a real dog match, the kind that still draws its rules from old issues of the *Police Gazette*, there's a ring about fourteen feet square. Each side has a line in the dirt, a scratch line. You set the dogs behind their scratch lines and hold on to their collars good and tight. You let them go. Each time there's a break in the action you pull those dogs apart and put them back behind their scratch lines. If one of the dogs doesn't scratch the earth, running in place to get back into it, the fight is over. No dog fights that doesn't want it. It has to more than want it: it has to claw for it, it has to want it like the fight was a chunk of steak or a piece of pussy.

When a dog doesn't scratch, the fight is over. A dog that gives up, you call that a cur. Dogs that don't have any cur in them, we call them game dogs. Dogs that scratch even when they're close to death, who'd rather die than give up, you call those dogs dead game.

But you don't let them die, not if you're a real dogman. A dead-game dog is the goal, the pinnacle of a pit dog. That needs to breed. To make more dead-game dogs. To breed more warrior stock. You've got to be the quit for a dog that doesn't have quit in it. A man who lets a dead-game dog fight to the death is both cruel and foolish.

My employer is a cruel and foolish man.

You may think that I am cruel and foolish too. Maybe you want to think I'm the villain of this story. And maybe I am. But now I'm going to tell you about Lucy. And hers is a story worth telling.

The hotel where I have built my emergency room sits in one of those Detroit neighborhoods where it looks like a slow-motion bomb has been exploding for the last thirty years. Even the people are torn apart. I see crutches, wheelchairs, missing limbs. Nothing and no one are complete.

I pull off of Van Dyke into the lot of the Coral Court. Hookers, tricks, and pimps scatter like chickens. The tires crunch on asphalt chunks and broken glass. I park as close to the room as I can.

I leave Lucy in the cab of the truck and open the door to the room I have rented. It is just how I left it. One of the double beds has been stripped down, a fresh sheet of my own laid across it. I crank the thermostat up to max. Lucy will need the heat.

I wrap Lucy in a towel and carry her across the lot. She is so small and so cold. As we cross the lot, a fat man drinking from a brown paper bag shoots me a look.

"Goddamn, what'd you do to that dog?"

"Put your eyes back in your head, motherfucker," I tell him. He looks away. So cur he can't even see I'm bluffing.

I take Lucy inside. I place her on the sheet. The white sheet blushes as it soaks up her blood. I open up the tackle box that serves as my mobile medical kit. I change the gauze on her neck. I tape it on tight. I take out a long loop of bootlace. I tourniquet the front leg, the one with the most bleeders. I take out a brown plastic bottle of hydrogen peroxide. I yank out the marlinspike on my knife and stab through the lid. I wash out the wounds. Dozens of punctures, tears, jaw-shaped rings all over the front of her.

They say that Vlad the Impaler walked through the hospitals after battle, inspecting the wounded. Those with wounds to the front of them got promoted. Those with wounds in their backs, like they'd been fleeing, Vlad had those men killed. Vlad would have made Lucy a general. Her back and haunches are unmarred. She'd fought every second she'd been in the bout.

Tough little bitch. Proud little warrior.

The match had been in an abandoned warehouse—no shortage of those here. The ring had been built in the morning out of a two-foot-tall square of wood filled up halfway with dirt. Around the ring stood gangbangers, bikers, cholos, and mobbed-up types. Dog matches in Detroit are like those ads by that one clothes company that always have the black guy and the white guy holding hands, except at the dog match the other hand is filled with blood money or a gun.

Tuna was owned by Frankie Arno, who lived in St. Clair Shores along with all the other Detroit dagos who didn't get the memo that the Mafia doesn't run things anymore. His dogman was Deets from the Cass Corridor. Deets doesn't hold to the old ways. Deets uses a homemade electric chair to fry his curs, and hangs live cats from chains for his dogs to chew on and improve their grips. When the referee told us that Tuna came in heavy, I told Jesse to kill the match.

"Four pounds is too much," I told him.

"Fuck that," Jesse said. "You told me this bitch is game."

He was a short man with a short man's temper. He was the only man I've ever known to lose money in the drug trade. He bought Lucy and some other prime stock when he was flush. He also hired the best dogman in Michigan, if you don't mind me calling myself that. Now that he was down, he was looking to recoup his investment. I do not know who he owes money to, only that they are frightening to this frightening man. This type of fear doesn't make a man listen to reason. I tried anyway.

"She is," I said. "She has potential to be a grand champion. That's worth more money than one fight."

"I'm not bitching out here. I'm not a punk."

Across the ring, Deets studied us behind hooded eyes. Deets knew Jesse needed the purse money. Deets knew that I wouldn't be able to talk Jesse out of the match if Deets brought his dog in heavy. Four pounds wasn't a mistake. It was strategy. I had to hand it to him. He'd played it beautifully. I gave him a nod to let him know. He just kept staring back.

Before a match, each side's handlers wash the other one's dog. Keeps a man like Deets from soaking his dog's fur with poison. Back in the old days, the rule was you could ask to taste a man's dog if you were suspicious. I didn't like handling Tuna, much less licking her. I know the signs of a dog who has been treated mean. When I washed her she trembled, and a deep growl burbled in her chest. It sounded like a boat idling at the dock. Pit dogs shouldn't growl at a man. We breed them to love us. I didn't want to know what Deets had done to her to ruin that. She kept growling but she didn't bite me. Maybe it would have been better if she had. If she'd bit we'd have put her down right there. That's one way our world and the straight world agree: dogs that attack men have to go.

But instead I took Lucy to one end of the ring and Deets took Tuna to the other end. Lucy, who had licked my face with a dog's smile just a minute before, strained to get away from me to head into the fight. The fight is a pit dog's highest purpose. We have bred them to not feel fear or pain. We have bred them to have wide jaws and a low center of gravity. A pit dog wants the fight the way a ratter wants the rat, the way a bloodhound wants the scent. A dead-game dog wants it more than it wants life.

On the signal from the referee I released my hold on Lucy. The two dogs collided with a slap and the sound of snapping teeth. Otherwise the warehouse was quiet. The spectators at a dog match are like the men at a strip club. Sometimes they cheer and clap, but mostly they stare on in silence, lost in their own private world.

In the fight there's nothing for a handler to do but watch. You can't teach a pit dog to fight any more than you can teach a horse to run. You exercise the dog, but the dog teaches itself.

There are many ways of dogfighting, styles as different as tiger style and monkey style in those old kung fu movies. Some dogs are leg biters. Some go for the head. Some dogs use muscle and buzz-saw speed, while others fight smart. Some just latch onto the bottom jaw and hang on until the other dog burns itself out and gives up. Some dogs are killers whose opponents don't get the chance to give up. They tear throats and end lives.

Tuna was a killer. She went for the throat. She had a good, strong mouth that tore Lucy up. She had four pounds on her, enough to bully her into position.

Lucy was the smartest dog I ever saw in the pit. She rode Tuna around, denied her the killing grip. Lucy turned the overweight bitch into a leg-biter. But Lucy couldn't get her own holds to stick. Tuna muscled out of them each time. Thirty minutes into the fight Tuna worked herself out of Lucy's grasp and sank her jaws into Lucy's neck. She shook Lucy, trying for a tighter grip, and Lucy slid under her, got her claws into Tuna's belly and twisted herself free. As the dogs repositioned them-selves, bloody, winded, I told Jesse to pick Lucy up. The fight was over, I told him.

"Are you fucking kidding me?" Jesse asked. "No way."

I could have picked her up then. I should have. But I didn't.

It took her another half hour and maybe her life, but Lucy fi-nally broke the bigger dog. When Tuna went cur and we pulled Lucy off her, Lucy was still clawing to get at the beaten dog.

Tough little bitch. Proud little warrior.

It wasn't until later, while Jesse counted his money, that the adrenaline went away and Lucy collapsed.

If she pisses, she lives. So I need to get fluids into her system. I take out a plastic bag of saline. I stick it under my armpit to warm it up for a minute. I hook the IV up onto the metal stand.

I take Lucy's leg in my hand and roll my thumb around it until the vein is visible against the bone of the leg. I wipe Lucy down with an alcohol swab. I get the IV needle out. I go to put the needle in. I stop.

My hand is shaking. I stare at it for long seconds. I take a few deep breaths. The shaking subsides. I slide the needle in. I secure it with horse tape. I take the IV bag out of my armpit and hook it to the IV.

Next I give Lucy a shot of an anti-inflammatory drug, pre-measured for twenty milligrams per kilogram of bodyweight. Next, penicillin, one cc per twenty pounds of body weight. While the fluids go in her, I get back to treating her wounds. I trim the hanging skin to keep the flesh from going proud. I check her mouth to see if she has bitten through her lips. Her gums are the whitish pink of fresh veal. Better. Not good enough.

I close the wounds. Some bites just get a little powder. I get out the staple gun for the worst of them. They bind the wounds together with a great loud CLICK. Lucy does not wince or whine while the staples snap down on her flesh.

Tough little bitch. Proud little warrior.

I will not let her die. But there's nothing I can do now. I have to give the fluids a chance to work. She sleeps. I can't. I watch bad teevee, something with fat people sweating on treadmills. I switch channels. People screaming at each other, throwing glasses, throwing punches. I switch again. The news, nothing but lying politicians and pretty dead white girls.

A knock at the door. I check out the peephole. It's Jesse. I open the door. A miasma of whiskey-stink comes in with him. He looks at Lucy. He whistles a low note.

"She still living?"

"For now."

"Do what you can, man," he says. "She's hardcore. Me likey."

"She'll be a hell of a dam," I say. I'm talking too fast. I never was a salesman. "Let's breed her with that brindle stud that Lopez has . . ."

"Hell, no, not yet. Bitch has fights in her yet."

"Jesse, she'll never come back all the way from this," I say. "She's already going to be a legend. Four pounds under and the dead-game bitch won. Breed her."

"She's going back in the pit," he says. I chew a chunk out of the side of my mouth.

"That rapper dude who was there, the one who owns Cherry? He wants to match her," Jesse says. "Shit, man, Cherry's a grand champion. She's legit."

"Lucy's leg won't ever heal right. She can't win another fight."

"Fuck it, then we lay money on her to lose. It's still getting paid."

I don't say anything. My hands are shaking again. I don't want Jesse to see.

"Palmer?" He looks at me.

"She can't go back in the pit," I tell him. I try to sound calm and steady.

"What's this can't shit?" Jesse turns his body sideways. It's an unconscious reaction of a fighting man to a threat. You turn sideways to make your body a smaller target to your enemy. I think about the stories I've heard. The things Jesse's done to men who cross him. Stories with knives in them. Pliers. Heated pieces of metal.

There is a scratch line in front of me.

I do not scratch. I do not fight.

"I'm your dogman," I tell him. "You're the owner. You make the call. If she lives, Jesse. Big if."

His posture goes back to normal. He smiles.

"That's the spirit. If she dies, she dies. But if not, patch her up and we match her against Cherry. The gate will be enormous. Anyway, I didn't get into this to be a breeder, like some bored Grosse Pointe housewife with her goddamn Pekinese. I'm in it for the blood. Win or lose it's a payday, isn't it?"

I say, "Yeah."

Cur. Goddamn cur.

Jesse leaves. I look toward Lucy. Lucy's ribs rise and fall so gently. If she lives, she will not recover fast enough. She will lose her next match. Lucy is dead game. She will not quit until she is dead. And Jesse won't pull her out.

If she pisses, she lives. But then what? She fights. She dies. Dies bad.

I'm saving her life to kill her in a month.

Tough little bitch. Proud little warrior.

I'm sorry I am not as strong as you.

At the bottom of the tackle box is the final treatment. Vets call it T-61. It's a fatal mixture of narcotics and paralytics, legally available only to licensed veterinarians. If I inject the T-61 into the IV bag, Lucy never has to wake up again. I take the plastic stopper off of the T-61.

The IV continues its drip-drip-drip. Lucy stirs. Her legs run in dog dreaming, swaddling up the blanket around her. She snarls. She bites the air. Still fighting in her sleep.

Still fighting.

Okay then. We'll do it her way.

I carry Lucy out into the parking lot and put her down. She sniffs the ground weakly. Her paws shake with the effort. She looks up at me with pleading eyes. She knows what I want of her. But she is so very tired. She falls into the gravel. Some of her wounds open up again. Blood drips, but no piss.

I'm talking to her. I don't know when I started. I don't know exactly what I tell her, but I know that it is true. The world fades out around us until we are the only two things left in it. I make her a promise. I know that I mean it. I will not let her die.

Lucy squats. My heart sits too large in my chest. It kicks and kicks. Lucy yelps. She squirts hot amber piss onto the parking lot. A flood of it.

Tough little bitch. Proud little warrior.

When she is done Lucy limps over to my side and leans against me, confused by the noises I can't help making. I stand in the hotel parking lot and cry over a puddle of dog piss.

I made her a promise. I will keep it. Lucy will not fight again. She's fought enough. Me? I'm just getting started. If Jesse has a problem with that, he better be ready to scratch.

I WISH THEY NEVER NAMED HIM MAD DOG

Some people will tell you that a person's name has power and meaning. But it's not so. A name's just a name is all. It don't have the power to affect your fate. Maybe you think it's because I'm named Geat myself that I have this opinion. Here's what being named Geat means: it means that my daddy was one hardcore Aryan son of a bitch is what it means. But just because I'm named after a bunch of white barbarians don't make me a natural-born Super White Man. Here in the Ozarks, people here being mostly white as an albino's scalp, you go around hating the niggers and Jews, you might as well get a hate-on for the Martians. There's plenty of pale-ass bastards around here to hate anyway. Of course, if you can't keep yourself out of prison like my old man, you might run into a few more of the brothers.

That's why my name is Geat Mashburn and also why I always had two birthday parties when I was a kid—one in the Leavenworth visiting room. See, the things that happen, the choices folk make, those are the things that shape you, not a name. But nicknames are different. A nickname stuck to you at the right time can twist your life around forever. Most people who you'd ask about Mad Dog McClure, they'd tell you he was so cussed mean and crazy that God himself had that name written down for him in the Book of Life. But most of those people don't know what I do. See, I was there.

I was there at Jackie Blue's the night Joe got the name Mad Dog. When the night started, he was just Joe McClure, a good old boy with a job sticking rebar in concrete. The guy was a metalhead with shaggy hair, usually wearing some black T-shirt with a name like Morbid Angel or Cannibal Corpse on it, but that's not that strange in these parts. He was a big fellow, almost as tall as me, but in a way you wouldn't notice. No jailhouse tats, nothing in the world that would have made you think that this fellow was going to become one of the most feared men in the hills.

To tell the truth, the only guy with a rep that night at Jackie Blue's—except old Jackie himself—was me. See, I'm a watchdog. Around here we don't have no Mafia or big crime families to keep the peace between operators, or to police 'em when they try to run games on each other. So if you want to make sure your deal goes down without a hitch, you call on me, and I'll come along to watchdog the deal. People see me coming their way and all their thoughts of double-crossing and dirty deals just dribble out their ears like creek water.

The night in question I was drinking double Crown and Cokes and talking to Jackie about what Mike Lewis had done

last weekend in the parking lot of the bar. See, the weekend before old Mike Lewis got off at the bus stop down at the square
having just come from a seven-year bit for armed robbery and
walked straight to Jackie Blue's to drink away his gate money.
About six Wild Turkeys later, Lewis bumps into some square
john who'd just walked into the wrong bar looking for a place to
watch the Cards game. Now understand when a man walks out
of a seven-year stretch, he's different than when he went in. In
this case Lewis done swoll up like a tick and covered his arms in
dirty gray tats of the Grim Reaper, FTW, the number 13, and
the like. So the square john was real apologetic, tried to buy
Lewis a replacement for his spilled drink.

Lewis just went sort of crazy, talking about how this square
john was talking out the side of his neck and whatnot. Jackie
tells him to take it outside. Even Lewis knew not to start shit
inside Jackie Blue's—Jackie's retired, but he likes to stay ac-
tive—so he drags this little square john outside and gives him
an old-fashioned Ozarks ass-whipping. And when he's done, he
props the fellow up against the side of the car and makes the
guy open his mouth. And then he pulls out his pecker and takes
a leak using that fellow's mouth for a urinal.

So the next weekend, Jackie and I are hashing the story
over and having a laugh. Maybe it seems a little cold to laugh
at it, but you learn quick in the life that you either laugh at the
fucked-up shit around you or you start doing it yourself. Is the
square world like that too? Anyway, me and Jackie had a big old
time telling each other the story, and we never paid any mind to
Joe McClure playing the Ms. Pac-Man machine in the corner.

Maybe twenty minutes later, who walks into Jackie Blue's but
old Mike Lewis himself, looking like a week out of stir hasn't
taken the edge off his crazy. He orders three double Wild Turkeys in three minutes and pays for each of them with a twenty

as fresh and clean as a new-snowed field. It doesn't take Magnum, P.I. to figure that Lewis ran out of the gate money they gave him when he got set free and that he's robbing gas stations again. Mike Lewis was waving Jackie over to order number four when he got interrupted.

"Cocksucker!" Joe yelled at the machine, and then he slapped the glass top. A ghost must have got him. But since the song on the jukebox died at just that second, Joe's swearing comes out louder than he meant it to. You know how that is. For some reason no one will ever know, Lewis gets the idea that Joe went and called him a cocksucker. Like I said, prison can change a man, and sometimes things happen that you don't ever tell no one about. So Lewis walks over and shoves Joe right out of his chair, just like that.

Joe's hammer spilled out his tool belt of its own accord. He didn't fish it out like you've heard it told. And most of the people at Jackie Blue's that night didn't know that Joe had just spent twenty minutes listening to the story of how Lewis turned a man into his private piss pot just the week before. So I guess to them, when they saw Joe come up from the floor and open up Lewis's head with the claw end of the hammer, it might have looked unprovoked. And I can see how if you didn't know the whole story, the way Joe turned the hammer around and gave Lewis a few more whacks on the way down could have looked like overkill.

Well, Jackie Blue's cleared out pretty quick after that, and I left along with everyone else, not needing that kind of shit in my life, so I can't tell you what Joe's face looked like while he watched old Mike Lewis drip blood onto the scummed-up carpet. But I've often wondered on it.

And it wasn't but a week later that I heard someone call Joe McClure Mad Dog for the first time.

"You hear about old Mad Dog, what he done last night?" Bill Houser asked and then wiped chaw spit off his flavor-saver. Houser is one of those good old boys always has a plastic cup with him half full of black sputum. Makes me sick. The cash he was paying me to sit in a holler and watch some fellows move bales of weed from one truck to another made it tolerable.

"Mad Dog?" I sliced a bite off an apple, ate it, and wiped off my knife. Down at the bottom of the blade is carved a cross, followed by the word white, the signature of the old boy who made it for me. Crosswhite's a good blade, and the old hardass who made 'em died a few years back, so I keep it sharp and clean.

"Who the hell is Mad Dog?" I asked, pushing the knife back in my boot.

"That dude what put the hurt on Mike Lewis. Mad Dog McClure."

"Joe McClure?" I asked. "Since when is he called Mad Dog?"

"I ain't ever heard him called anything but. Anyhow, last night I guess he was over at the Pink Lady, shooting Jäger down on pervert row. He'd gotten himself a favorite—a slice by the name of Sunshine, and not a bad choice neither. The crank ain't reached her face yet like most of the scags down there. Anyhow, Mad Dog's throwing his money on the table and getting a face full of fish in return, and some dumb son of a bitch who'd drove down from Monet starts bitching about how Sunshine isn't giving him the old tuna special. Guess he got mad enough to go ahead and call that stripper a whore, which ain't exactly like calling the Virgin Mary one, but still I guess—"

A bang shook us both from the story. I had my sawed-off up off the bumper and raised before I could see that it was just a fellow who dropped the plastic-wrapped bale he was hauling. I sat back. Houser laughed.

"You all right?" he asked me. "Seem a mite bit jumpy."

"Just tell the story. McClure's stripper gets called a name, and . . ."

"Well, what do you think happens? Mad Dog gets out that hammer of his he carries like he's just some dumb construction worker—"

"Well, that he is."

Houser waved this off, rolling his eyes like I'm the stupid one.

"Sure he is. Guess that's why he took that hammer and turned that boy's front teeth to fairy dust floating in the air." He mimed a tomahawk chop. "Then he went after the dude's friends, all three of 'em at a time, and I heard he had two of them on the ground and the third one balls-out running by the time the bouncers got to him."

Houser shook his head and swirled his spit cup.

"Can't believe you ain't heard it yet—a mean hombre like yourself ought to know about what the other hardcases are up to."

To tell the truth, I didn't give much credit to the story—chaw juice isn't the only type of shit known to dribble out Houser's mouth. But over the next couple of months the hits kept coming. Stories about Mad Dog—and it was always Mad Dog in the telling, never Joe—trickled down and around. Mad Dog smashed the window out of a fellow's truck and dragged him out to stomp him in the parking lot at Remington's. Mad Dog and Sunshine—who I guess got smitten when he pulverized that fellow's incisors—smashing empties against the wall of the Dew Drop with no one there brave enough to say boo about it. Mad Dog cracking the arm of some rent-a-cop down at the Ozarks Empire Fair—he got pulled in on that one, but I never heard nothing coming of it.

All this time I didn't see the fellow, as Jackie banned him

from the bar after that action with Lewis and I'm pretty loyal about where I do my boozing. But one night I ended up at a little roadhouse just outside of town on account of having just watchdogged a deal out on a farm. It wasn't the biggest deal I ever saw go down—just a bunch of trembling suckmouthed peckerwoods each scared of their own shadow—but work had been slow as of late. I needed a drink when the deal was done.

I didn't recognize him at first, and might not have at all if he hadn't been sitting with some other fellows from the life that I knew. I shook a few hands before I turned to this fellow in the black tank top.

"Hello, Geat."

Well, what a few months and a new name can do. He'd grown a tangled billy goat beard, for one. For two there was a tattoo—still wet looking—of a slavering pit bull on his bicep. You could see by the way he was sitting and the way everyone else was sitting that he was the fellow in charge. Maybe helping that out was the woman at his side, who I guessed was Sunshine. She was a pretty little thing all right, but she looked at me with that half-lidded kind of look that I've learned to stay away from. Both of them looked pretty tricked out with flashy jewelry— diamonds on her fingers, another in his earlobe—and clean clothes. Mad Dog McClure wasn't hauling rebar for his scratch no more, that much was clear.

"Hello, Joe," I say back.

"It's Mad Dog these days," he says back, twisting his trunk so that the tattoo faced me.

"Course it is," I say, and take out my wallet and turn to face the bartender. "How about a round for everyone here—and let's get some shots with that. How's Wild Turkey sound to a Mad Dog?"

He smiled and leaned back in his seat like he'd won something.

"Sounds right, Geat. It sounds right."

So we did our shots and drank our beers while people played pool and stuck quarters in the jukebox and played those songs that I guess it's required by law that you hear every time you step into a bar out here: "Gimme Three Steps," "Thunderstruck," "If You Want to Get to Heaven," shit like that. I mostly sat back and watched the rest of the table slobber all over Mad Dog's ass. He tried to play it cool, but I could see it plain there behind his mask—he was stone hooked on being Mad Dog. After a while he got up to piss. A minute later I went over to the jukebox like I was thinking of playing a song. When he came out the pisser I waved him over.

"What can I do you for, Geat? If you're looking for good music on that juke, forget it. Just that same old redneck shit in there."

I didn't have no idea how to do this. None at all. But it had to be done—somebody had to try to save this boy's life.

"Look, Joe—"

"Mad Dog."

Shit. I'd blown it already.

"Mad Dog, look, man, I just—shit You need to cut this shit out, amigo."

He laughed like he didn't know what I was talking about, but I could see it in his eyes.

"Cut what shit, Geat? What shit exactly should I cut out?"

"You need to get back to your crew and haul some mother-fucking rebar and cut out this 'Mad Dog' shit. You are not . . . this isn't you, man. This is not going to end well."

"Aw, fuck all that. You think I'm going to sit back and let y'all have all the fun? Think I want to keep getting to the job site at five in the goddamn A.M.? Come on, Geat, I'm not Joe McClure anymore. My name's Mad Dog, see?"

He tapped his fingers on that hammerhead on his tool belt. I looked back and saw that the table was staring at us. I turned back, palms up. Chill out, the hands said.

"All right there, Mad Dog. Look, I understand, I do. But I always thought you were a good fellow back at Jackie Blue's, and I don't really want to see no harm come to you. You keep pumping yourself up like this and some shark is going to come by and take you down just so they can have people say, 'He's the one who killed Mad Dog.' You just think about it, okay?"

I turned to get going, and one of his boys stood up to meet me on the way out, a rat-faced fellow by the name of Webby. He kind of sneered at me, and my first instinct was to rear back and bitch-slap him. Instead, I turned back to Mad Dog.

"Care to put a leash on your boy?" Mad Dog laughed and waved Webby back in his seat.

"No hard feelings, Geat. But when you next see old Jackie, you tell him that I don't take too kindly to being banned, hear?"

"Now that's a message that you can deliver yourself, if that's what you want," I told him, heading out the door. I was talking to a dead man who wasn't smart enough to know it yet—a man who'd try to send a message like that to old Jackie Blue. I wish they never named that boy Mad Dog.

A few weeks later I got a call from Ricky Beal, a fellow who cooks up Nazi dope down around Fair Grove. He told me that him and Bill Houser were planning up "a big ole swap." I knew what he meant—they'd trade a couple of ounces of meth for a bale of Houser's weed, simple as can be. They did it every once in a while, and they'd done business enough that they mostly didn't even bother with me riding along.

"Well, I don't mind it," I told him, "just so long as you know that I do all of Houser's watchdogging and that's not a problem for you. Either way, no one's going to rip no one off on my watch."

"Yeah, well, that's the thing here, Geat. I guess you ain't heard yet, but Houser done found himself a new watchdog, much as I hate to tell you. And seeing as how I don't know his new guy, I thought I better bring you along."

Now that I thought about it, I hadn't heard from Houser in a few months. I hated to hear he'd found someone new, though—he was good for quite a bit of my green. It happened every once in a while, though, when someone thought they could save a little money by going outside my circle. Never bothered me none, as those folks usually ended up getting ripped off on the other guy's watch. One way or another.

"Geat? Geat, you there?"

"What? Oh, sure. Sure, I don't mind coming along. Say, what's the name of that new fellow Houser got?"

"Shit, man, it's Mad Dog McClure. See why I want a little muscle on my side?"

Bill Houser's place sat on a couple of acres just outside Busiek State Forest. Houser didn't grow his weed on his land. He grew it on the government's. More than that, the weed he grew he didn't sell here. He bought Mexican shit weed off the I-44 pipeline and sold that around here, and moved his bud north up the pipeline to Chicago where he could get real money for manicured smoke. The trade was some of his homegrown for some of Ricky Beal's Nazi dope.

Mad Dog was late—I knew he would be—and me and Ricky and Houser leaned against the house playing with the dogs. They'd each brought two men with them for doing the heavy lifting and for just a little more comfort. I turned down the beer Houser offered, but those boys had several.

"Now, Geat," Houser said as he drew back the beer I'd waved off, "I hope that there's not any bad blood between us, what with me giving Mad Dog a day in court."

"Variety is the spice of life," I said. "No hard feelings at all."

You could hear Mad Dog coming before you could see him. That kind of frog-throat heavy metal that he liked came roaring up the driveway, like he had some kind of devil choir announcing him. The car was one of those little Japanese things with a spoiler on it, red with black flames crawling up the hood. He parked it next to my old truck and got out with a pump shotgun in his hands and that hammer still hanging from his belt. He nodded and swung the shotgun up on his shoulders as he walked our way. I bet the others saw what he wanted them to see, the bad guy making his entrance to the movie. I saw the joy kidlike behind his eyes.

"Evening, boys."

"I told you eight thirty," Houser said.

"And I ain't but ten minutes late, so what?" Mad Dog gave Houser a glare. Houser might have asked what the point of a watchdog was if he wasn't there before the merchandise, or he might have said how I had been there almost an hour already. But all he did was look down and give that cup of his a little more spit. I pushed one of the dogs away from me and stood up.

"Hey there, Mad Dog. Good to see you."

"Same, Geat."

"Boys," I said to the rest, "before this goes down, me and Mad Dog are going to step inside the house and go over a couple of ground rules.

"Ground rules?" Houser asked. "What all is that? I don't recall nothing about there needing to be ground rules."

"And I don't remember you ever being around when a swap's

had two watchdogs," I said. "It ain't the normal way, and I know an old hand like Mad Dog can see it clear enough."

I took the pistol out of my waistband and tossed it in the gravel. Mad Dog took the hint and laid his shotgun up against the house as he followed me inside. I turned around once we were inside so that Mad Dog had to shut the door and lean against it to face me. Once we were inside, he gave me a smile.

"Man, this is a fucking rush. You've got the life, Geat, for real."

"That I do."

"You ain't really got any ground rules, right? I mean, look, Geat, if this is about that night in the bar, my buddy was being a jerk. I told him off. I'm awful sorry about the whole thing. Friends?"

And he held his hand out to me.

"I'm awful sorry, too," I said. I kicked him in the chest. My boot hit him flush. He went back and took the door outside with him.

"Holy shit!" someone yelled as I came through the empty doorway. The dogs started up howling. Mad Dog looked up at the stars, struggling for breath. He fumbled his hammer out of his belt. I mashed his hand against the gravel. He screamed. I went down on his chest and pulled out my Crosswhite blade. I looked down at his face and there wasn't a Mad Dog there. Just Joe McClure. I put the blade in behind his collarbone and pushed down until you couldn't see the cross on the blade. I locked eyes with him. First there was fear and then there was pain and then there was knowing and then there was nothing.

I wiped the blade on his shirt as I stood.

"Boys, we've got a deal to do, then I got a piece of trash to dump out in the forest."

Houser dropped his spit cup so the brown gunk splashed out. In the moonlight it looked a lot like Joe's blood.

"He killed Mad Dog. Geat killed Mad Dog McClure."

That was what he said. And I knew that pretty soon that was what everyone would be saying. The power of that name would come to me, the way it does for a cannibal who eats his enemy's heart.

"Geat killed Mad Dog McClure."

I am sorry that they named that boy Mad Dog. But I don't blame you if you don't believe me now.

PLAYING DEAD

We got greedy, every one of us. Greed's fine. Greed gets you up in the morning. But we got soft, too. That's how Birdie catches us slipping.

Sloppy. All the coke is laid out on the table. Sloppy. Kody's on watch with his gun on the other side of the room. Sloppy. I never got that dead bolt that Devin told me to get. It was just a matter of time.

It happens fast. One second we're talking shit and cutting the coke with vitamin B. The next the door explodes and the Port Side Massive comes through. Big bad Birdie leads the way with an AK pointed at my head. I don't recognize the rest, aside from Birdie's brother Little Bird, and I can't decipher their yells. The yardies talk in that Jamaican patois, thick syllables that bounce off American ears. But anybody can translate a gun to the head. In the front room a couple of them toss the six keys of coke into duffel bags. They make me, Kody, Skinny, and Dap strip down butt-ass naked. They yank the gold right off our necks, even yank the fronts off Skinny's teeth. They herd us into the bathroom, into the clawfoot tub. I press up against the tiles so my crotch don't dangle against Skinny's fat ass in front of me.

"Move you backsides, Brooklyn boys," Birdie says as he herds us into the tub, dropping enough of the accent so we can understand. "Don't need no cuss-cuss nor fuckery. Come an' get baptized, now."

He pushes Skinny aside with the barrel of the gun to get in my face. His eyes are the color of old hard-boiled eggs. His dreads hang woolly and thick. Even in the stank-ass bathroom, his smell of ganja sweat and grease cuts through.

"Oi, it be Liver Johnson." Birdie taps my skull with the barrel. "Big 'bout you, mon. Tell me, Mr. Liver—where I be finding you bloodclot friend Devin? I can't find no hide nor hair of the bumbaclot boy."

The crack game in Brooklyn ran smooth through '92, at least compared to the craziness up north in Queens. Then the Jamaicans showed up last year. I'm talking real island boys, not the Fat Cat crew from Jamaica, Queens. The Jamaicans don't play nice. They drop bodies and rip off anything they can grab. Don Gorgon ran the Port Side Massive up until last week. Devin caught him slipping outside a curry-goat shack on Fulton. Gorgon had ripped off a safe house like this one near MDC Brooklyn, and Devin put a sunroof in his dome for his troubles. Back a week Birdie was just Gorgon's number one rudeboy. Now he's in charge. He ought to say thanks.

"I don't know where Devin's at," I say, "and that's real." It's true, not that I'd say different if it weren't. "That shit's between him and you. You want to jack us, jack us, but I'm not snitching to you any more than I'm going to snitch to the cops."

He splits a smile, but it doesn't touch those rotten eyes.

"If ya kyann catch Quaco, ya catch him shirt," Birdie says, pouring the island sounds on thick. But I understand and my guts turn to water. I thought maybe this was just a scare tactic, herding us naked into the bathroom like this. But it's not.

"Nigga, what? What shirt?" Kody asks. I could tell him, but I'm too busy getting set to die. I'm not ready.

Birdie turns on the shower. We jump and bump each other in the ice-cold spray. I press against the tiles. Skinny's big ass shimmies. I don't want to look, but that's all I get in my field of vision, and I don't want to die with my eyes closed. It's Auntie Ruth who brings me back down from the hysteria. She's going to find out that I got put down in a safe house bathtub, bare-ass and dead in a pile of coke-slingers. Scandalous.

Kody turns around and it's like he wants to say something like I'm sorry or Make it stop, but he doesn't. Shit, I'm not mad at him for not covering the door. Not one of us had a gat bigger than a .32. What were we going do when five yardies with AKs bust through the door but die? Over Skinny's shoulder I see Birdie spit something to his brother, Little Bird. Birdie walks out of the room. His brother raises his machine pistol.

"Drop them bloodclots," Birdie says.

Just before everything explodes, Skinny barks a laugh.

"Shit, little nigga, bring it."

The world goes thundercloud.

"If you can't catch Quaco, you catch his shirt." Devin says as he's opening the trunk. Six keys of pure base in a duffel bag waits for me. It's the last six before Devin goes underground.

With the Port Side Massive gunning hard for him, he knows his shelf life on the street is milk-short. "That's what those goat-eatin' motherfuckers say."

"Quaco?" I ask. "Who names somebody Quaco?"

"I know I'm not hearing you talk that shit. Who named you Liver?"

"You did, motherfucker," I say, and then we're laughing. They call me Liver because I'm high yellow as a motherfucker, with a white mom and all, so back in the day Devin said I looked jaundiced. A bunch of the kids on the block had to run to the dictionary before they laughed at that one.

"Let it slide," he says. "Quaco ain't the point here."

"All right, then. If you got a point, lay it out."

"It means if you can't catch a slippery motherfucker, you catch what you can reach. Put a hurt on his homies, his pad, his family and shit. Don't matter if they did anything wrong or not. If you can't catch Quaco, you catch his shirt. You see what I'm saying?"

"You saying that you got beef with the Port Side, and you plan on getting real slippery. So if these dreadlock motherfuckers can't get at you, they're coming to get at me?"

"Liver, I ain't promising you they gonna come. I'm just saying, it's in the realm of possibilities. It's no secret that you and I put in work together. I ain't trying to fuck with you. If I knew these motherfuckers got so damn tribal, I might have thought twice before lighting up Don Gorgon. I'm telling everyone I know to watch out. Don't get a big head over it."

He gave it to me straight up. I don't blame him. I'm a grown-ass man and I could have taken care of myself. But deep down I never thought the posse would come for me. Last week I thought I was going live forever. Now I'm counting seconds.

* * *

Skinny saves my life three times. The first time was when he opened his mouth just before the yardies light us up. Every single one of them starts the killing with him. When the first claps come, I just drop. Bullets puff plaster and tiles over my head, but none of them touch me. That's the second way Skinny saves my life. Motherfucker is so big that none of the yardies see that they don't hit me. The third way Skinny saves me—wait on it.

Skinny's head hits the wall while most of him falls on top of me. My breath goes out. More weight crashes on my legs. I smash my nose against the tub floor. It's gritty. No one's cleaned this tub in an age. The shooting stops for the time it takes me to take one gasp of air and then it starts again, bullets raking the pile. One shot, slowed from going through Skinny, clangs loud against the side of the tub so close I can smell it. Each second I think it's over, but nothing stops. There's smoke and blood and booms and stench and mist and white noise from the showerhead.

I'm not even grazed. The bodies on top of me shudder the last drops of life out of them. I wish those yardies turned the water warm. Not because I'm cold, I'm way past worrying about that, but because I can feel the difference between the cold water and the blood dripping hot off the corpses of my friends. A weight slams down, pressing my face harder against the floor of the tub. Dap fell out onto the floor when they turned him to a rag doll, and now they dump him back in. He empties like a tipped garbage pail.

I try to listen. These boys have done their dirt. Now all they have to do is pack up the coke and hit the road. I can play dead until they leave. Then I find Devin and we go hunting for the rest of our days. Show these yardies what a war is. Just as soon as they leave. Just as soon as—

The water rises. Some part of Kody blocks the drain. Shit's

been inching up and now it's starting to fill my nose. If I twist my head, then Skinny on top of me will shift and the yardies might see it and do some double-checking. My arm's extended over my head. I move it sloooow.

"What you mean I'm'a stay and watch them boys?" It sounds like Little Bird. "Bumbaclots going nowhere—dead don't walk."

"Yeah, them boys is going to move." That's older brother Birdie. "Them coming with us, once we fix them right. Got to get them ready for travel—for easy packing. The rest of us is goin' to make a run to get the tools."

Water plugs my nostrils—it takes all I've got to stop from blowing out. I take little tastes of air with the high side of my mouth. I've got less than a minute before that's gone too.

"What tools?" Bird asks.

Kody's forearm blocks the drain. I get my hand under, so it's my palm blocking the drain. It might slurp and that'll get Birdie and Little Bird's attention. Or might not. I tense up and get ready to chance it.

"Cutlasses. Machetes. We going take these Brooklyn boys to pieces and leave Devin with a mystery, see? So you sit tight, little rudeboy, until we come back with the proper."

The drain slurps, one quick burst. I piss one warm trickle. My breath comes back in short hard draws as I wait for Birdie to come poking. But there's nothing but the shower static.

I can't make out much in the front room. It sounds like it happens the way Birdie said. Him and the posse leave to get carving tools to chop up me and the boys like jerk chicken. I'm blind and half deaf at the bottom of the tub with no idea if Little Bird is out on the stoop or sitting on the shitter three feet away. But I do know they left him with something, which puts him up on me.

But now's better than never, and never is showing up when Birdie comes back with the machetes. You can't play dead through a dismemberment. My body's aching all over from ice water and dead weight all pressing on me. I pull in my arm, playing Twister with stiffs. My elbow pops—I wait for the bullets—the bullets don't come. I raise up from under Skinny, not looking at his face. His half-a-face. I break out to the surface. Pushing Skinny aside sets something loose. He barks a death rattle. For a second I think it's mine. I look around. The bathroom is empty. I live a few more minutes at least.

I'm standing in the spray, stepping out of the tub. Our clothes are gone. The yardies stole my drawers. The door is open. I can't see Little Bird. I'm looking for something to split his dome. Looking and seeing nothing. I don't have long. Birdie has to have his machetes stashed someplace. I don't think the yardies are at the hardware store shopping right now. I take a peek through the doorway. Little Bird's sitting in the same chair I was in thirty minutes ago with his back to me. He thinks any threat to him is coming through the door, not from the tub full of corpses. Maybe he's right. Back in the bathroom I can't find anything to kill him with. I could rip off the towel rack, but it's flimsy fake brass. There's one old toothbrush. It'd work to shove that through the eyeball straight into the brain, but that's crazy kung fu shit and I can't take that kind of chance. That leaves a bottle of shampoo and a dirty-ass towel. Even covered in the blood of my friends I can't think of anything murderous to do with a shampoo bottle, so that leaves the towel.

I soak the towel over Dap's body. I twist it tight into a rope and come creeping on Little Bird. My feet stick as I go through the kitchen. We kept it sloppy here. Real sloppy. But that's over now. I cross my arms, slip the towel over Little Bird's neck, and straighten my elbows like I'm ripping something apart. He claws at it. He makes noises like a busted radiator. He kicks his life out onto the dirty linoleum.

His drawers got piss in them, so I wear his baggy jeans commando and slip on the fat flannel shirt. Baggy gear means everything fits everybody. I'm ready to make a break for it when I hear Birdie and his men coming back. Dance hall garbage from the car stereo gives them away. I think quick, stuff Little Bird's hat with newspaper like it's full of dreads. They left Little Bird holding a MAC-10. I check it. Locked and loaded. I step to the midnight air just as the yardies roll up. In the dark they just see the Rasta shape standing in the doorway, not my liver skin.

I light them up. Bap-bap-bap-bap-bap. I don't run. In this part of Brooklyn, cops wouldn't check out a mushroom cloud. I come up slow, covering them—if one of them is playing dead, that'd be some funny shit. Pot smoke snakes out the bullet holes—the yardies went out so high they might not know they're dead yet. I jerk open the door. The dome light shines through a film of blood and brains onto three dead yardies. Three. No Birdie.

Well, fuck that shit, I think, I'll see that nigga another day, and I start to break out—and then stop.

If you can't catch Quaco, you catch his shirt. When they find the bodies of Kody, Dap, and Skinny back there in the tub, not cut up, and my body nowhere to be found, Birdie can do the math. He knows me. He'll figure me for a playacting motherfucker who rose from the dead to cap his brother.

I wanted to know who Quaco was, and now he's me. I'm him. And if Birdie can't catch me, he catch my shirt. Auntie Ruth, my cousin Kianna, friends from grade school I don't even remember. Birdie will kill them all now that I've smoked Little Bird.

I can't have it. Maybe Devin can live with his shit spilling all over the damn place, but not me. I'll chew on this MAC before I let that happen. And I realize that maybe that's my only choice. Leave myself just one more body in this big pile that's growing bigger by the minute. Better that than what happens if Birdie finds out I'm alive.

If they find the other three bodies. But if I make Skinny and the boys disappear the way Birdie wanted us to be gone, Birdie won't have a fucking clue what happened, and he sure won't figure I raised up from the dead. Let him put Little Bird on Devin. That's where it belongs in the first place. Make it look like they caught me, and they won't have to look to catch my shirt. If I do what I'm thinking I have to do, it means that I play dead for real. This life would be as over as if I'd caught one back in that bathroom. It means being a ghost. I already feel like one.

I reach past the dead yardie driver and pop the trunk to get the machete. Turns out Birdie was being poetic with that word. It's a chainsaw back there. I pick it up and head to the house. I hate to think about what I'm going back in there to do. But shit, they're all dead in that bathtub anyhow. They won't ever know what I'm going to do to them. They won't feel a thing. And now Skinny gets to save my sorry-ass life one more time.

RED HAIR AND
BLACK LEATHER

She had an ass like a heart turned upside down and torn in half, and that's what you call foreshadowing, friend. It was a slow Wednesday afternoon at the bar and in walks this gal, red hair pouring over her shoulders, wearing a wifebeater and black leather pants. And all of the sudden the Cards game on the tee-vee didn't seem so interesting.

"Nice place."

She pulled herself onto a stool in front of me, thumping a big leather purse onto the stool next to her. Strictly speaking, what she said was a lie. Jackie Blue's isn't much to look at, brick and linoleum, bars on the only window up front, old neon signs on the wall. But still it sounded like she meant it. She had a southern lilt, not that twang that you get around here, and it made whatever she said sound like sunshine and kittens.

"Thanks."

"It yours?"

"Indeed it is."

"Well, I guess that makes you Jackie Blue, am I right?"

"Well, I'm Jackie, anyway," I said. I haven't answered to Jackie Blue in a long time.

"Jackie Blue . . . Isn't that the name of a song?"

"By the Ozark Mountain Daredevils, as a matter of fact. You find yourself in the Queen City of the Ozarks just now, if you didn't know it." She wrinkled her nose at that.

"Is that where I am? I had wondered. I hope you don't mind me saying, she doesn't look much like a queen."

"Well, take a look 'round the rest of the Ozarks and get back to me on that."

She dropped a smile on me that peeled about twenty years off my old hide. That might have put me about even with her.

"Jolene," she said, and put out a freckled hand for me to take. It felt hot to the touch.

"Well now, that's the name of a song as well, right?" She groaned a little at this—I guessed she wasn't a Dolly Parton fan.

"What can I do you for, Jolene?" I asked.

"I'll take a Wild Turkey neat with a Dr. Pepper back, if you please."

That is a drink order that makes a man sit up and take notice. I poured the liquor in a highball glass and filled a twin for myself. Owning a bar you want to watch things like drinking in the day. But there's exceptions for everything, and this was shaping into an exceptional day. She took a hard swallow of the Turkey. I could see it play havoc with the muscles in her throat, but it never touched her face.

"So now, Jolene, seeing as how you don't know where you are, maybe it's a pointless question, but what brings you to town?"

She smiled, but this time there was a little crack to it, like there was something that wasn't a smile underneath. She put her hand on her purse like it was fitting to fly off, then dug in it for some of those skinny toothpick cigarettes that ladies sometimes smoke.

"Jackie, I'll tell you what it is. I'm in town for exactly two reasons. One's to drink Wild Turkey. The other is to get laid."

I've had it every other way I can think of, but I've never had it served to me sizzling on a platter like that. Nobody ever has it that easy, I'd bet, other than the rich, the famous, and the folks in porno movies. There was something there in the back of the skull telling me that God made up his mind long ago that I'm not that lucky and the strings you can't see usually turn to chains. But sometimes you got to jump just 'cause the chasm is there. Hell, what was I going to do, go back to watching the Cards?

I topped my glass to the rim, then hers. Then I held up that near-full bottle of Wild Turkey up between us and poured the whole thing into the sink.

"Fresh out of Wild Turkey," I told her.

She laid that smile on me again and it peeled off another couple of years so that now she was the older one, the one in charge.

"Maybe you want to close up shop early," she said, sliding off the stool.

"Maybe I do."

I walked around the bar, hoping she couldn't see me tenting out my jeans. I threw the dead bolt on the front door and pulled the strings on the blinds on the window. Before I did I peeked out into the parking lot, which was empty except my old truck.

Maybe she parked down the street, I figured, and turned to ask her. The words got jammed in my mouth. She was in the corner of the bar, sitting on the glass top of the sit-down Ms. Pac-Man machine. I wondered if her ass was cold, seeing as how while my back was turned she'd stripped out of those black leather pants. "I thought this would be fine," she said, patting the video game table under her ass. It was fine, all right. Fine, indeed.

And time passed slowly and well, the way it did back when I was young and it seemed like everything would last forever. Every now and then someone would rattle the door, as the regulars who couldn't believe I would shut the door came calling. A few times the phone rang, and I knew that had to be some right thirsty boys indeed who'd go home to look the number up to see if they could rouse me. But none of the noise bothered us at all, except once, later on after the sun set and there wasn't any light but the orange glow of the Budweiser clock over the bar. A noise like a long loud rip of fabric went by. It was the sound of a motorcycle, something chopped and mufflerless. At that, Jolene stiffened under me like a deer that hears the step of a clumsy hunter. But then it passed and faded and after a few seconds she unlocked her joints and turned back to a slippery slick she-devil. Where there'd been fear in her eyes, I saw only thunder.

So we talked and then we'd wrestle some more, and then talk again. She told me about growing up in Georgia, about how her grandmother was an honest-to-God dirt eater who'd scoop soil off the ground and pop it in her mouth. She told me about how football was king then and how she'd put her prom dress on layaway. She told me more than that, and I noticed that none of her stories ever reached up into the past few years. What had happened to her since that prom stayed a mystery.

And I talked too, and if she really listened she might have noticed that I did just the opposite. Everything I told her was in the now, ever since I opened Jackie Blue's. Mostly stories about what the drunks did, like the time Mad Dog McClure opened up Mike Lewis's head with a claw hammer not a foot from where we now lay. Stories about bad men, but I didn't delve back into the dark days back when I was bad myself.

So when we talked, we kept our secrets. But when we weren't talking, there were no lies between us, and she saw me for who I used to be. A dangerous man. And I saw her as a woman in danger. So much danger. I got it in my head that maybe I was the man to get her out, and then I thought maybe that was just what she wanted me to think.

We slept on a bed of our clothes and woke around dawn to birdsong outside. It was a sound that didn't fit in Jackie Blue's any more than if you heard Lynyrd Skynyrd coming out of the treetops. God, she still looked good in that morning light, and let me tell you: that was a thing I wasn't used to anymore. A man who owns himself a bar don't hardly ever need to go to bed alone, but what you wake up with is usually a poisoned head and possum bait smiling next to you, the kind you'd chew your arm off to get away from. But not her. I stared at her until my old eyes started to burn, and then I took some time to look at me instead. The fur on my chest and belly had all faded from black to gray over the last few years, like I'd spent the time soaking in hot water and the color had leached on out. The gut had gotten bigger, but I hadn't gone soft. No, not yet. Under the faded india ink tattoos on my forearm I still had some ropes of muscle from hauling kegs and tossing drunks. Maybe I wasn't just Jackie the bartender yet. Maybe there was still some Jackie Blue underneath, ready to bark at the moon.

She turned herself over, blinking in the sunlight, just as I was finished pulling on my old leather boots.

"Good morning, cowboy," she said, not bothering to cover herself in the daylight. "Sorry to see you've already got yourself dressed. A lot of effort for nothing, if you ask me."

"Protein," I said. "This old goat needs protein if he's planning on walking, much less working, today. There's a diner down a block, should be opening about now. How do you like your eggs?"

She sat up and hugged herself, as if all the sudden she knew she was naked. Then she slipped that mask back on and leaned back to show herself, pale skin against the leather pants beneath her.

"I'll put you to work, Daddy," she said. "All you need is a little bit of that popcorn and a belt of brown stuff to get you back in the saddle. What do you say?"

Lord, even after the night she'd gave me there was something in me kicking its heels up for more. But I picked up my keys, partways because I truly needed some grub, and partways to force her hand. It was time to get some truth from the little lady.

"Over easy suit you?" I jingled my keys at her.

"Don't go."

See, there was some of that honesty she showed me on the floor last night.

"Why not?" She hugged herself tight again.

"I need you. I need shelter, don't you see?"

"You hiding from a man?"

She laughed.

"I suppose you could say it that way. I prefer calling him a low-down son of a bitch."

"And what's this son of a bitch want with a pretty little lady like yourself?"

"Can't you guess it?" She stood up in all her glory. "The dummy thinks we're still in love."

She's right. It's a story I can believe. That don't mean I do, just yet.

"This dude got a name?"

"Cole."

"Cole? Just plain old Cole? Like Slash or Cher?"

"That's all I know to call him."

"That's all you know? And you're his woman?"

"Was. As of last night, I'm all my own again."

She'd met him in Tulsa, she said, and picked up with him and his boys. Bikers—called themselves the Iron Horde. That name meant something to me from stories I'd heard from some of my meaner customers. Oklahoma boys who moved Nazi dope up and down I-44.

"Cole weren't a Nazi," she said.

I shook my head.

"I'm not saying the boys are Nazis. The dope is. You ain't never heard of Nazi meth? Some good old boy from around these parts, around twenty years ago, he went over to the library over at the local college and found the recipe that the Nazis had for cooking up amphetamines back in World War Two. It's the premier recipe for Ozarks meth. Our little contribution to that world."

She nodded, like something in her head just clicked. She pulled her purse close to her and then stood up to pull on her leather pants. It pained me to see her do it, even if it was fun to watch.

"I don't know about Nazi dope," she said. "What I do know

is I'll take a whole lot of lip off a man if he's as much fun as Cole was, but I'll be damned if I'll let him put his hands on me. Last night, Cole had a little bike trouble; the ride had gotten real bumpy. We were all pulled over on the side of the exit, just where the highway is up the road?"

I nodded to let her know I knew where she meant. That was only a quarter mile from here.

"Well, I asked Cole when we'd be heading back to Oklahoma. Now, I'd ridden with him long enough to know that I came in a weak second place to that bike of his. But I guess I never saw it in him to smack me around like that."

She touched the side of her face, turning it toward me to examine. It looked flawless to me.

"And that was that, huh?"

"I jumped the guardrail and marched through a couple of yards and then saw your place and grabbed that there barstool and figured I'd start up a new life right then and there."

"Is that what you figured? You didn't walk into here like a woman on the run. You walked in like a goddamn cannonball."

She smiled.

"Ain't you ever cut free of something and it made you feel wild?"

Not for a while, would be the truth of it. Not since I walked out of the life and into this bar. But the way she said it, and the way she looked, made me think that maybe I could do it again.

"Think that motorcycle man is still looking for you? That why you don't want for me to leave?"

She stepped closer, put a hand on my arm. The whiteness of her made my skin look dirty.

"You ever dump a mean son of a bitch?"

I pushed her hand away and grabbed onto the bar.

"Is he coming? Is that why you're here?"

"I figured if he was coming, he'd come right away. It wasn't until I thought it was safe that I made my move with you. You see?"

I did. I saw that Jackie Blue's was on a back road, and while it might be the first place you'd find on foot, it'd be real easy to miss from the road, especially if Springfield weren't your town. And I saw that she knew that, and that she hadn't given that fellow near enough time to give up on her before the two of us got busy. But I also saw that it'd been near fifteen hours since she came through the door, and even as fine as she was, fifteen hours is longer than a man could look for a woman with his buddies in tow.

"If he were coming, he'd'a been here by now," I said. "So there ain't no harm in me running to get us some breakfast. You can keep laying low here, and then the two of us can sit and figure out what the next part of your grand adventure is going to be once you leave here."

"That's what you want?"

I wanted to run across the room and mash myself to her. I wanted to sell the bar and buy a bike and see how far across the planet it could get us. I wanted to shave the gray out of my hair and step back into my old boots and stomp and steal for enough money for us to last forever.

"Yeah," I told her. "That's what I want."

I drove over to the Pancake House and ordered up some grub. I picked up a paper and took a seat, turning straight to the editorial page to read the letters from the loonies. There was one about how abortion stops a beating heart, one about how the school board was trying to teach kids evolution, or, as the letter put it, "from goo to you via the zoo." The last letter was about how the Ten Commandments needed to be posted up in every school. All three quoted the Bible in the first paragraph.

"Jackie?"

I looked up and there was Pinkle. Don Pinkle, that is, looking every bit the methed-out redneck that he was. He stood there dope skinny with a sad, scraggly goatee and bags under his eyes that looked like full-grown slugs. If he'd slept in forty-eight hours, it had been forty-eight hours ago. He flashed me a smile, but that isn't the right word, because there wasn't nothing flashing in that meth mouth of his. Teeth yellow and orange and brown like dry dog food. He came by the bar some nights with some of the boys, every once in a while getting on a construction crew to get an honest dollar, which must have felt lonely and out of place in his wallet. He never tipped on a drink, not once.

"Pinkle," I said like it was the whole conversation, and tried to get back to my newspaper. But he wasn't having it.

"Went by the bar last night."

"Did you now?"

"Wasn't open."

I dropped the paper, seeing as it was clear he wasn't going away.

"Now, Pinkle, don't you think I know that?"

"Knocked on the door and everything."

"Trust in your senses, son. We were closed."

"Thought I heard voices," he said, scratching a scratched-up face. His nostrils stood out bloodred and ragged against the trout belly of his skin. "That's why I knocked, see. But nobody answered."

"Heard voices? You? You can't tell me that hearing voices is some sort of strange occurrence in your life. Not with the shit you've got floating in that lump of gristle you probably call a head. I bet it sounds like happy hour in there most times."

"I thought maybe you were in there with someone, is all," he said, trying to give me a saucy look.

I stood up fast and took pleasure in how he scurried back a few steps. Sometimes folks forget just how big I am, or what I used to be able to do. Sometimes I forget myself.

"And I thought," I said, "that what I do in there or don't do is exactly one hundred percent none of your goddamn business. Care to tell me how I got so misled about that?"

Just then a waitress called out, saying Pinkle's food was ready and that mine was getting bagged up.

"That's a whole lot of food for a body," he said as the waitress put my two bags on the counter. "Got yourself a tapeworm?"

"Got something to plug that hole I'm getting ready to stomp into your head?" I asked back.

"Not meaning to aggravate you," he said, holding up his palms.

So I took a few deep breaths and told myself that the dumb twidderpated motherfucker was too stupid to barely breathe, much less know when to leave well enough alone.

I was wrong, it turns out. Pinkle really is stupid, just not as stupid as I gave him credit for. Not that I figured it out by his next move, which was to try to pay for his breakfast with a hundred-dollar bill. It was early yet and of course the joint couldn't handle that, so I groaned and paid for his while mine was still being put together. I didn't even ask where he'd gotten the hundred. I didn't want to know.

"Could you throw in a dollar extra?" he asked me with a sheepish grin. "I need me some quarters."

"You need to be laying off that dope," I told him, but pushed the quarters across anyway. "And you need to not think about setting foot in Jackie Blue's until you're ready to pay me back, hear?"

He grabbed his food and hotfooted out the door. I went back to the waitress, who was kind of cute, and gave her a wink. Well, the goat had really woke up, hadn't he?

"Some dude, huh?"

"Yeah, people suck," she said. "Bank on it."

"Rosy disposition."

God, I wish I knew what it was about girls with too much eyeliner and a bad attitude that got to me. Then I thought of Jolene grabbing the brass pole that ran under the bar and I knew that I was good to go again.

"Mister," she said, pushing my bag of food over to me, "work the night shift at a diner some time, and then you can tell me about how great people are. Especially people like that one."

I was about to tell her about how I worked a bar and knew how people could be when it struck me that there was something strange in the way she'd said "like that one."

She stressed the *that* like she could still see him, so I turned around, and there he was at the gas station across the street, jabbering into a pay phone. I didn't like that. And then I remembered that hundred-dollar bill, and I liked it all even less. There was plenty of ways that a man like Pinkle could get some cash money, none of them nice. But to have a fresh hundred to spend on breakfast at the end of a binge, that didn't set right. It was probably nothing, I thought, but decided I'd walk over there and see what he had to say. And then he looked up and saw me crossing the street and dropped the phone. A piece of paper fluttered to the ground in his wake.

A big semi rolled past the road and by the time it passed, Pinkle had a good head start, and besides, I wasn't going to win no footrace with a meth head. I stopped at the phone and picked up the paper scrap. Then I dropped the breakfast. There was an out-of-town phone number scrawled on it, with one word under it.

Cole.

The chopper was a beauty, all silver fire and wheels. It slouched in front of the front door of Jackie Blue's, which hung open. The wood around the doorknob was splintered like someone had kicked it open. He couldn't have been there long. Less than ten minutes had passed since Pinkle made his call. In fact, when I climbed out of the truck I could still hear the bike's engine ticking. Then that sound was ripped out of my ears by a scream coming out the door. I ran inside, my fists balled at my sides, hoping he didn't have a gun.

He probably had a gun.

The inside of the bar looked like someone had picked the whole place up, turned it upside down, and given it a shake. The register was popped open and the cash drawer hung crookedly out, the shelf lifted to search out the underneath. Bottles had been shoved off the shelf, some of them breaking on the floor. A cloud of booze stung my eyes and plugged my nose. All this came to me out of the sides of my mind. Right there in the foreground was a big old boy with an arm inked with jailhouse tats wrapped around Jolene's throat. His other hand muffled the screams with his palm. Jolene's eyes bulged out over his hand, and her own hands didn't fight his but instead clutched her black leather purse.

"Just stand back there, pops," he said with an Oklahoma twang. "Keep a cool head and we can all walk out of this."

"Funny words coming from a man just trashed my bar."

He barked a little laugh at that.

"Brother, I just got here. This little bitch," and he gave her a shake for emphasis, "is the fucking source of all our troubles, yours and mine. I don't know how she's been playing you, but if I had to guess, I think I could. I know how she suckered me."

He took his arm away from her throat and cupped the crotch of her leather pants. She tried to say something through his other hand, but it kept it muffled.

"Played me but good, brother, and now she's playing you. When I came through that door she'd done cleaned your register out."

I took a step forward. The place was cleaned out, all right.

"You really Jackie Blue?" Cole asked.

For the first time in a long time, I said yes.

He shook his head sort of sad like.

"Well, that's what I get for opening my big fat mouth. I done told this cooze enough stories about Jackie Blue back in the day to fill her head with 'em. See, my pops used to ride through here, and he always told me that back then the hardest man in the hills was Jackie Blue. And so when we'd ride by, I'd always have to tell this bitch here about it. I guess I might have oversold you and made Jolene here get some mighty bad ideas."

She tried to shake her head, but I could see it was true. She'd known just who I was the moment she'd walked through the door. Makes sense. Lucky is just what you call someone when you don't know how smart they are.

"That may be," I said, "but still all the same, if a gal wants to take her leave of you, it's best to let 'em go without a fuss. What do you say?"

He laughed and yanked Jolene's purse out of her hands. He shook it and it dumped out on the floor, and first out came all my money that she stole and then came pinkish-white bricks, one two three.

"Brother," he said as I watched the Nazi dope pile on the floor, "it ain't the leaving so much as the stealing that bothers me."

Well, damn.

"All right," I said. "I see it now. She done played you and then she played me. Figures. So you take what's yours and get on out and we'll call it a day. How's that sound?"

"Sounds fine," he said, then turned to Jolene. "Scoop that shit up—leave Jackie Blue's money—and let's get going. Let you have one last ride before you get yours."

"No," I said. "You don't get it. The lady stays."

He looked at me like I gone plumb crazy.

"Jackie, I know she's got a snatch like hot butter, but come on—this bitch is pure poison. You can't want her to stick around after she tried to rob the both of us."

That's so. But as much as I might like to see it, I can't let him hurt her. See, even if it was partway, or even in total, a lie, that girl made me wake up last night—she made me see who I am.

"Sorry, son," I say to him. "But one way or another you're taking your hands off her."

The fear hit his eyes and I thought it was going to be easy, but then the fear went away. At first I wasn't sure why, but it's that his young ears heard it before mine did. The sound of a group of motorcycles rolling down the road.

"Now Jackie, I got all sorts of respect for you, but I got to think of my own rep too. Can't let my boys think I got taken by a slut and a geezer."

He reached behind him and pulled a little flat pistol. He moved the girl in front of him, as a shield like. His boys were rolling into the lot. I had about fifteen seconds to make it right.

I walked in stepping to the right, putting Jolene totally between us. That suited him fine, he thinks, as I'm not going to hurt the woman. But also it meant he can't see me clear to shoot me. I took Jolene's head in my hands—our eyes met and

I laughed—and I slammed her skull straight back into Cole's nose. He dropped and just for a second I stood holding Jolene by the head like I was getting ready to lay a Hollywood kiss on her. But instead I tossed her to the side so I could stomp Cole while he was down. Three times did nicely. Then I picked up the pistol with my right and his shaggy greasy hair with my left and I dragged him to the door, just in time for his three buddies to come to full stops on their bikes. The dust swirled up and their engines roared and I stepped into the storm of it all, dragging Cole behind me. By God, I felt good.

"Welcome to Jackie Blue's," I said.

PLAN C

Shit.

Shit.

Shit.

Five people, plus me, here in the lobby. I've ushered the tellers from behind their stalls. One hot number in a green dress, one cow-eyed woman with a cat on her coffee mug. So that's two. Three is this wrinkled old fart in a sweat-stank security guard uniform. Four is the lone customer, some kid wearing a leather jacket, black like mine. Number five is Mister Suit, Mister Push the Button, Mister Brains All over the Fucking Floor. I told him in and out in two minutes and no one gets hurt.

I told him. Maybe he was a little hard of hearing. Don't push the button. He pushed the button. So I swabbed out his fucking earwax with a Q-Tip of the gods. If he'd listened, there wouldn't be the five cop cars outside and I wouldn't be playing eenie-meeny-miney-hostage. He pushed me to Plan B.

The two teller women sob, the young guy looks like he wants to bad, and the old man sits with a look on his face like I got up every day of my life for this?

"I don't want to die," the teller in green, the pretty one, says. She says it again.

"Anybody here who does want to die?" I ask. "A show of hands. No one? Okay, we'll just consider that a given from now on, so there's no use saying it anymore. Behave and we all go home tonight."

The cop cars all face us, the doors open like wings and the cops crouching behind like baby birds. Baby birds with guns. And one's got a bullhorn and he says something but the alarm is still ringing and there are glass doors between us so whatever he says comes out wah-wah-woh-wah like Charlie Brown's teacher. It's okay; I know what they're saying: come out with your hands up and forget about that bag of money and we'll overlook that capital murder charge puking blood on the floor behind you.

Wah-woh-wah is right.

All right, eenie-meeny-miney-moe to the green-dress teller. The cow-faced one looks relieved, like finally, not having a man look twice at her is paying off. Like every stay-at-home Saturday and second of loneliness was worth it. Because now she gets to have more of them.

I admit it. I'll look better on the evening news with this green dress next to me. A gun to her head and a bag of cash in hand, holding her tight to me. Fucking rock-and-roll album cover, right?

"Let's go," I say as I take her by the hand. "Everyone else, sit tight, right, and don't even think of running."

I walk the green dress into the sunshine and insanity. So

many guns cock it sounds like maracas. Helicopter white noise. live teevee with the overhead view, more cameras across the street. And me with blood on my face. I hope someone is taping this, McGuire or someone else at the Mayfield saying oh, shit, that's Tyler.

Wah-wah-woh-wah the cop with the bullhorn says, and I could understand him if I tried. But we aren't bargaining here. I've got four hostages, I've got time, they've got nothing I care about. I want a car, I want no one following me and the girl. They'll send helicopters after me, sure, and if they didn't the teevee guys would. But Plan B is worked out for that. Wait and see.

So I yell what I want. Twice. Three times. "Drop the guns," I yell, "or I'll do her."

She flinches away from the promise of her death. It knocks me off balance a bit, and then where her head used to be, where mine was a second ago: pink mist. I never even hear the shot, just the pop of her head. I drop her. She falls like a sack.

Sniper.

I pull the trigger copwards, firing behind my back as I make for the door. Little gusts of hard wind puff past me. Chunks of concrete dance at my feet. I get in the door somehow, the three hostages on their feet, ready to run but frozen.

"Whoa, whoa, whoa," I say, "we're all back to square one, so let's have a seat and think over our options."

I do ugly math. Three hostages. Someone over at the precinct is going to get a talking-to tonight about that pretty little head-shot thing in the green dress. Oh, yes, someone is going to convene a panel, maybe even a committee, over that young woman bleeding out next to that bag of cash. The bag of cash on the sidewalk.

Shit.

Shit.

Shit.

I dropped it when I dropped her. Maybe twenty grand if I'm lucky. I didn't have time to count it. I was going to count it later, hiding in the storm drain off I-70, waiting for McGuire or whoever to come pick me up and put me in the trunk of their car.

I need that money back in here with me, and then I can start looking for another way out. The roof maybe, or an air duct or something. Plan B just needs a little break to still work.

I point the pistol at the young dude and say, "Hey, guess what, get out there and grab my cash. And if you run, I kill one of these nice people here, understand?"

He shakes his head at me idiot style, so I break his nose with the gun butt. I have three people's blood on me and it's not even noon.

"Now you get out there, grab the bag, and back in. Do it in five seconds and you'll be the first one I let walk. Promise."

So he goes out the door and he doesn't get two seconds before they light him up.

Shit.

Shit.

Shit.

And the cops kill their second hostage of the day. They saw a leather jacket that looks like mine and a bloody face and someone gave the okay and down the dude goes.

I blast a few shots out the window. The charging cops thought I was dead. They freeze and retreat. None drop. Man, if I'm in this thick, I think, I'd like to tag a cop. Just might yet. "On your feet, old man," I say, and his face hasn't moved yet, like he got bad Botox: get the paralysis, keep the wrinkles. "I need that bag. You walk out slow, they'll see you for who you are, you walk back in. You fuck it up and I pull the trigger on her." I point the gun. Cue the teller's squeal. "And then I shoot you in the back. Understand?"

Maybe your adrenaline dries up when you're old or maybe this bastard has huge old balls, because he doesn't flinch or frown or even blink: just nods. And stands. And walks.

Out the door, check. No shots fired, check. He picks up the bag, check. And starts walking toward the cops.

Shit.

Shit.

Shit.

I keep my word and pop the girl goes down. I turn the gun to the old man's back, bang bang both wide, then click click click. Dry. The old man makes it to the cops. My money goes with him.

No cash. No hostages. Not long before the cops do the math and figure what that adds up to.

I pull my spare clip from my pocket. Plan C. I had to work out Plan B; Plan C comes ready-made. It's there on every job I've ever pulled. I slide in the clip. Wild Bunch time. Butch Cassidy time. Hope a few cops splatter before that last freeze frame.

Shit.

Shit.

Shit.

BEAUTIFUL TRASH

They meet over the body of a beautiful dead boy. Green likes her right away. Her hands don't shake. She doesn't make bad jokes or cry or act cold. A lot of people wouldn't handle their fear so well. After all, it is her first corpse.

Gray November skies loom in the giant windows behind them. Manhattan babbles four stories below them.

She says her name is Sarah.

"Green Daniels," he says back.

They shake hands. Her hand is small. It is cold. The other hand fingers the red scarf covered in grinning yellow skulls knotted at her neck. Green gets it. She realizes how inappropriate the skulls are. But she doesn't want to draw attention to it by taking off the scarf.

"Victor sent you," she says.

UNSAID: You're the cleaner.

Green nods. Victor had called Green from L.A., from the law office in Beverly Hills that he never seems to leave.

"Cleanup on aisle seven," Victor had said when Green answered his phone. Victor left the rest UNSAID. UNSAID is their second language. He didn't use the word *dead*. He didn't use the beautiful dead boy's name. He gave Green the address and hung up the phone.

Green squats down to look at the beautiful dead boy. He flashes back through the past three years: The rise of a beautiful boy. Magazine covers, blockbusters, red carpets, paparazzi club shots.

And now this room: The fall of the beautiful dead boy. A bottle of OxyContin on the nightstand. The glass of watery whiskey next to the bottle. Downers and booze. The classic star-killer.

"Whose apartment is this?" Green asks.

Sarah hesitates. She tugs on her red skull scarf.

"Not his," Green says.

She nods. He picks up the prescription bottle and hands it to her. He points to the bottle's label. The name. A woman's name. A famous name.

"That's the thing?" Green asks.

"That's the thing."

"She's your client," he says.

"I'm her publicist," Sarah says. "One of them, anyway."

There are two kinds of publicists in this world. The kind who get good news out and the kind who keep secrets in. Sarah is the second type.

"She must keep you busy," Green says.

Sarah tries a smile at this. But it's like she's forgotten how to do it.

Green knows about her client. Everyone does. Young, rich, and famous for being famous. For putting her life on display. He's seen the client's face on a dozen magazine stands. He's seen her Brazilian-fresh vagina, thanks to an "accidental" up-skirt shot that hit the web two weeks before her last reality show came out. He knows who she's dated, and when. It doesn't matter that Green doesn't want to know. Everyone can't help but know. The knowing floats in the air like smog.

"She loaned him the place?" Green asks.

"He's in town shooting something. He's been here a week."

"How many of these does she have?" Green asks, shaking the Oxy bottle. He points to the label again. The bottle is from Florida.

"I don't know."

Florida is a doctor-shopper's paradise. Someone who braves its mosquitoes and white trash to get themselves a hillbilly heroin script doesn't get just one. They get several. Pure junkie logic. In Hollywood you could be an asshole, a fuckup, a junkie, a woman beater, whatever. As long as there was someone to foot the bill. The client can't handle another scandal. The insurance companies will bolt. When the insurance companies won't play ball anymore, that's when the roller coaster stops. A drug bust right now will ruin the client's career.

This is the job. Keep the client clean. They don't have to talk about it. They keep it UNSAID.

Green asks Sarah to give him the timeline. She breaks it down for him. A house cleaner found him first. A chain of phone calls followed: the client's manager, the agent, the head publicist. The publicist called Sarah. She told Sarah to call Victor. That's who Victor was: the guy you called while the body cooled.

No one called a paramedic. Everyone knew the drill. The

drill was UNSAID: he's dead and that's a shame, but there's no reason to bury the client.

"The house cleaner," Green says when she's finished, "legal or illegal?"

"Illegal," Sarah says.

"Piece of cake," Green says. "Talk to her. Tell her if she didn't see the body, she won't have to talk to anyone from the government. She won't have a problem with that."

Sarah nods.

"Here's what we're going to do," he says. "You're going to go down to that coffee shop down the street and order yourself one of those nine-dollar coffee drinks they have and you're going to drink it. You drink that coffee and tell yourself the story of you being the first one to find the body. When you can tell the story frontwards and backwards and out of order, come back here. I will be gone. Anything else your client wouldn't like the cops to find will be gone. The pills will be gone, except a few in his pants pocket. You will call nine-one-one. Don't try for an Oscar. Just make the call."

"Can we keep her name out of it?"

"It would take moving the body," he says. "Never try for miracles. That's when it all goes to hell. No, we can make it look like he brought his own drugs over here, and not give the cops any reason to question your client. Where is she, anyway?"

"She's hosting a nightclub opening in Vegas," Sarah says. "You wouldn't believe what they pay her to sit there and drink."

She tries another smile. This one works.

"Perfect," Green says. "Then she's got nothing to do with this."

Sarah nods and looks at the body. The smile goes away again.

"It's sad," she says. "Is it okay, what we're doing? Is it wrong?"

"You should get out," he says. "Of this business."

"Why?" She bristles, defiant, and Green likes her even more.

"You asked about right and wrong," he tells her.

Something stirs in Green as he watches her leave the apartment. Something he thought he'd drowned like a kitten in the bathtub a long time ago. He wants to call her back, to try to talk to her, try to make her laugh. But he doesn't. He tells himself it's because he has a job to do.

Green goes to work. He gets a garbage bag from the kitchen. He trashes the pill bottles. He finds the client's weed stash in green plastic bottles. The bottles have labels: Pure OG. Yoda. Lamb's Bread. LA Confidential. He trashes them. He wipes down surfaces. He finds the beautiful dead boy's phone on the ground near the bed. He goes through it. He checks the photos. He finds POV sex shots. The beautiful dead boy was a phone-hack scandal waiting to happen. Famous faces, famous bodies, famous smiles. Sarah's client, with dope-frosted eyes, spread-eagle on this very bed. Another starlet taken doggy style, looking back at the camera, back at the beautiful boy. Green deletes the pictures. He thinks twice and pockets the phone. Data is too easy to recover. Better to let the cops wonder where the phone got to than let the pictures leak out.

He carries the trash bag out with him. He steps over gray banks of filthy snow. He tosses the bag in a trash can near St. Marks Place and walks away.

He stays in a hotel room in Chinatown almost exactly the size of the queen-size bed, with water stains on the ceiling. New York City hisses and pops right outside the window. Fresh seafood dies on ice in the fish markets outside. The room has Internet and cable. He puts CNN on the teevee screen. He sets up on his laptop twin windows of Twitter and TMZ. He waits. He eats steamed dumplings from a stand around the corner. He gets used to the smell from outside. Green knows you can get used to almost anything.

Twitter gets it first. TMZ gets a picture of the body under a white sheet. Pretty soon after that the helicopters start buzzing the neighborhood. Constant chopper noises as news channels take meaningless aerial shots of the apartment building. The newscasters repeat themselves over and over, desperate to justify their existence. Green watches until he hears a CNN mouthpiece say Sarah's story word for word. The story will hold. The job is done.

Los Angeles in February. People wear sunglasses and heavy jackets. The beautiful day is cold to them. The body adjusts to paradise.

A man muscled like a gym trainer enters his West Hollywood apartment. The trainer turns on the light. Green sits in front of the trainer's computer. On the computer screen: a photo of the Most Famous Man in the World with a dick in his mouth. The trainer's dick. The trainer is getting deep-throated by a thirty-million-dollar mouth.

"Let me tell you where you fucked up," Green says.

The trainer tenses up, ready to run.

Green, UNSAID: I'll find you, and then I'll make you pay for running.

The trainer gets the message. He sits down.

"Let me tell you where you fucked up," Green says again. "You asked for too much money."

The American moviegoing public likes twenty-first-century special effects and 1950s moral standards. The American moviegoing public still can't stomach a leading man who likes the flavor of a good stiff prick in his mouth. The Most Famous Man in the World likes the flavor of a good stiff prick in his mouth. A photo of said suck job would spread like a virus through the Internet. Said suck job kills the Most Famous Man's salary quote. It kills his action franchise. It costs the Industry money. Said photo is valuable.

Unless you fuck up the play.

The trainer starts to say something. Green cuts him off.

"I don't know how much you asked for, and I don't care. All I know is, there's an amount you could have asked for and they would have paid it. But you cross a line, and it gets cheaper to hire me to make the problem go away. You being the problem."

Green doesn't feel anything while he hurts the man. He's not sure the man feels anything either.

Green walks out into the West Hollywood night. Blood on the front of his shirt. His phone vibrates in his pocket.

"Hey, Victor. It's done."

"Of course it is, champ. You're the fucking best."

Victor is honest by Hollywood fuckwad standards. His bullshit is so blatant it is a perverse form of telling the truth.

"I'm not calling to check in, baby," Victor says. "Cleanup on aisle seven. You have a badge someplace, right?"

The Grotto, the nicest no-tell hotel in the world. Green gives his key to the valet and walks up the famous pebble steps, the ones Jim Morrison fell down headfirst. He goes through the locked gate to the right, to the part of the hotel the wannabes and part-time party people never get to see. Heads down the steps to the swimming pool. Beautiful people. Young, naked, and free. Green stays out of the light.

Green knocks on the door of the bungalow. Sarah answers

the door. She is wearing her red skull scarf. She smiles when she sees him. Then she looks down and the smile goes away.

"You've got blood on your shirt," she says.

"Yeah."

He shows her the fake badge. Her smile goes fast. UNSAID: it's a bad scene.

"Sheriff's department, ma'am," he says loudly as he walks in.

A naked man with claw marks down his chest sits on the bed. Aaron Something-or-Other. An actor. He plays a doctor on some teevee show, one of those network shows where the hospital staff looks like a bunch of catalog models playing dress-up. He looks up at Green, disinterested and drunk. He looks back down at his hands. The knuckles are red, swollen.

Out of the bathroom walks a beautiful woman with a split lip. Her shirt is ripped. There is blood on her bra. She holds a fistful of ice to her eye. Green knows the look, the style. She is a pro, high end, the kind who hangs out at the bar at Beverly Hills steakhouses. Thousand bucks an hour or so, Green guesses from the look of her. She radiates something. It takes Green a minute to remember the name for it. Dignity.

"The son of a bitch hit me," the pro says. She takes the ice away from her eye. The eye is a tight purple swollen-shut bud, a flower before the bloom.

"She's a whore," Aaron says. UNSAID: whores are for hitting, aren't they?

Green takes a badge out of his coat pocket. He shows it around. The badge is made out of some cheap metal. It reads CHICAGO PD. Doesn't matter. The woman doesn't look too close.

Sarah stands in the corner. She fiddles with her scarf.

Green takes the pro to the bathroom. She sits on the marble countertop. She shows him her legs. Crisscross welts across her thighs. A mad pattern to the violence.

"What do you want out of this?" he asks her.

"Come on," she says, "he beat the shit out of me."

"You want me to take him in?" Green asks.

The pro looks at him. The pro, UNSAID: pretend I'm not a whore and tell me if you'd still ask that question.

"What's your name?" he asks her.

"Chablis," she says.

"What's your name?" he asks again.

"Caroline."

"Priors?"

She pauses.

"He pay you already?"

Caroline doesn't think. She touches her back pocket. Green reaches behind her and pulls out the envelope. He peeks inside. Looks like two grand in twenties. He hands it back to her. He gives her the talk—the talk a million real cops have given to a million bruised hookers. He tells her how it will go down. If he takes Aaron in, he'll have to take her in as well. He'll have to charge them both. Tears gather up in the purple split of her swollen eye.

"Now," he says, playing the world-weary cop, "are you sure you really want to press charges?"

He watches her think about it. About taking a stand. Then shakes her head no. Green has broken her.

Good job.

She nods. They walk back into the room. Aaron has put on some clothes. He has poured himself another drink. He has invaded Sarah's personal space. He touches her thigh. She squirms. Green clears his throat.

Aaron looks up at Green and Caroline. Grins.

"See you around," Aaron says as Caroline runs past Green and out the door. She holds in the sobs until she hits the doorway. The three of them stand still as her crying fades into the night. Sarah looks at Green. The look in her eyes. UNSAID: I don't have to ask if this is wrong.

Green holds the look. He'd done worse for less.

Aaron lights a cigarette as he tries to talk Sarah into staying. Actors are the last smokers left in Los Angeles. It keeps them thin. Green walks her out. They walk down a garden path toward the pool.

"I need a shower," Sarah says.

"It won't help," Green says. "But I know what will."

They follow the sounds of laughter to the outdoor bar. All these beautiful people. Green and Sarah find a table near the swimming pool. The drinks are eighteen dollars apiece. They have several. They charge them to Aaron's room. It's paid for by a studio, the one producing the animated film in which Aaron plays a love-crazed warthog. He's supposed to be doing press all weekend.

The landscaping rustles around them. Rats, Sarah says. They live in the plants around the hotel. They run wild in the Hollywood Hills. This afternoon she saw one fall out of the palm trees while a *Vanity Fair* writer interviewed Aaron. The thing lay dead for the full three hours of the interview. The staff didn't want to clean it up, afraid they'd draw attention to it.

"Smart," Green said. "It's the cover-up that gets you."

"It's getting me," she says. Her smile is real. Some of the thing they're carrying lifts off them then.

The waiter comes by to let them know it's last call. Sarah tells Green that the studio bought a second room for the night, sort of a green room for the press people. The other room is full of booze and food. Shame to let it go to waste. Green follows her to the room. He tries to remember how long it's been. A long time.

They drink. They swap stories. She tells him about getting a pedicure with the assistant of a reality star. The reality star is making a series about her upcoming wedding. Sarah tells Green how the girl told her there were cameras everywhere all the time, and the star and her fiancé never spoke to each other when the cameras were off. Nobody ever said anything about it. She tells Green how the Vietnamese ladies at the nail salon put their feet in bowls of tiny fish, tiny fish that fed off the dead skin of their feet. How the assistant watched the little fish nibble her toes while she said to Sarah, "I'm losing touch with reality. I don't even know what's real anymore." How the girl had been near tears. How the wedding show had been a hit.

Green tells her a story from the nineties, one of his first jobs in L.A. He worked a case for T——, back when he was still a name, before the drugs got him by the neck and took him down. T—— was the type of guy who figured that anyone with tits on their chest was woman enough to give him a blow job, no matter what they happened to have dangling between their legs. Green spent one hot and endless night cruising tranny row with T—— while the actor did lines of coke off the dashboard and lectured Green about twelve-step recovery. "What you need, Green," T—— had told him between coke shivers, "is to take a moral fucking inventory of yourself."

Green and Sarah both know about famous men who secretly died jerking off with belts around their necks. Autoerotic asphyxiation. It happens more often than you think. Green says those jobs are easy. Everyone will help the cover-up. Even cops. Cops find a guy with a belt around his neck and his cock in his hand, they hide the belt and call it an accident. Or at least they call it a suicide. David Carradine caught a bad break by dying in Bangkok, far away from the safety nets.

She pours. She talks. Nothing left UNSAID. She takes a moral fucking inventory. She tells him how she got her break as a scripty on a big sitcom. How the women on the set had a special place, a closet behind the craft services table. "What's it for?" she'd asked the PA who'd shown her around the set. "It's where we go to cry," the PA said. Sarah tells him that she'd laughed at that, thinking some women were weak. Some women gave the rest of them a bad name. Until the day one of the show's stars yelled at her for eight minutes because she'd brought the wrong cup for his coffee. She found the right cup. Then she found her way to the special place.

She tells Green about how she'd moved into PR, got a job at a big firm with offices on Wilshire. Three weeks into the new job her boss, a woman with cigarette-stained hands and an acid-peeled face, told her to give a blow job to a movie star they were handling. The woman told Sarah the star needed to relax before a press junket. It was part of the job, the woman had said. Sarah tells Green about the gleam in the woman's eyes. How some people get an evil done to them and they can't wait for their chance to pass it on to the next person in line.

Sarah had done what the woman asked of her, in a closet, on her knees. Sarah tells Green how it made her feel, like something hollow, like something you might keep your hats and umbrellas in. The star had texted with a buddy while she did it. He rested the phone on her head. Word got out. She got labeled. So she'd moved over. Switched to black-bag PR. A month later she met Green.

She tells Green about her last few months. She'd turned one actress's botched tit job into a struggle with cancer. A methfieled freak-out turned into exhaustion. She'd done a lot. But she'd never gotten back down on her knees.

She's quiet. UNSAID: it's your turn. Time for your moral inventory.

Green couldn't. Not yet.

She understands. She drains her glass. She comes across the room and she kisses him. He kisses back. He pulls away.

"Why me?" he asks her.

"Because," she says, "you're as scared as I am."

He knew she was different. She is the only one who has ever been able to tell.

They undress quickly. Everything else, slow. They are gentle with each other. They know they're both so bruised.

She gets up first. Green pretends to sleep as she crawls naked out of bed. He watches her dress through half-closed eyes. She is so beautiful, even now, hungover, her hair hanging in her face.

Back at his apartment he watches bad teevee in the dark. He orders pizza. He wonders if he should call her. He wonders where that would go. Could go.

He watches cable. An action movie from twenty years back. Oh yeah, movies. Somewhere right now in this town, grips move lights. Prop guys dig through their trailers looking for just the right prop. Actors do vocal exercises and learn their lines. Writers type. Scripties time scenes. The place where that happens seems a million miles away from Green. He is in a place in a faraway corner of that world, one of the places marked *Here Be There Dragons* on old maps.

He doesn't call Sarah. Not then, and not ever before it becomes too late. Sleep comes and the next day he is normal again.

He goes back to work. It's award show season. They always keep him busy.

Oscar night. Late. The helicopters have quit their endless loops above the intersection of Hollywood and Highland. Victor calls him. Victor says, "Cleanup on aisle seven."

"Okay," Green says.

"Can you handle some heavy stuff?"

Victor has never asked him that before.

"Yeah," Green says.

Green enters one of the Hollywood hotels. He takes the elevator to the eleventh floor. He goes to room 1103. He knocks. He listens. He takes gloves out of his pockets. He puts them on. He opens the door. He smells spilled champagne and something else, something wet and sharp and rich. His heart climbs into his throat and starts kicking. He turns on the light.

A body.

A skull-print scarf in a pool of blood, red on red.

Sarah's head is split open. Her eyes, once blue flowers, are now gray dull mushrooms. Her nails broken. The arms slashed. She fought. Fought hard.

Crisscross welts on her legs.

A mad pattern to the violence.

He cleans the scene as best he can. He wipes down surfaces. He tries not to look at her. But she's everywhere he turns.

While he cleans, he thinks. He makes a plan. He doesn't think Sarah would approve of it. But one thing he knows: he's done worse for less.

Green knows Aaron will be someplace he feels safe. He chases a hunch. He makes a call to confirm it. He drives to the Grotto.

He street-parks. He goes in the delivery entrance. He walks to the bungalow. He knocks.

"Yeah?"

"Let me in," Green says.

Aaron unbolts the door. He blinks at Green. Recognition comes slow.

"You're the guy," Aaron says. "The cleanup guy."

Aaron opens the door. He's wearing jeans and a T-shirt. His tuxedo lies crumpled on the floor.

"We've got to get you cleaned up," Green says.

"Why?"

"You know why."

Aaron smiles. It is flawless, charming, and Green cannot see the demon underneath.

"What do we do?" he asks Green. Green pokes his head into the bathroom, as if he's looking for hiding witnesses. He checks the shower. He yanks on the bar that holds the shower curtain up. It's solid. Five-star construction.

"Take a shower," Green says. "Take the shower of your life. I'll clean up around here. Leave your clothes out here so I can trash them."

Aaron strips in front of him, smiling.

"Do you want to know why?" he asks Green.

"I know why. She wouldn't get down on her knees for you."

"Not the way I'd put it," Aaron said. "But whatever. I want to know why you're here."

"I haven't picked my number yet," Green says. "But I want enough so I don't have to do this anymore."

"Doable," Aaron says. He goes into the bathroom. Green waits five minutes. He breathes slow. He thinks about Sarah and her scarf made out of skulls. Then he removes Aaron's belt from the pants he left on the floor. He tugs on the belt. Tests it.

It does not break. He takes off his shirt. He picks the belt back up. He pushes the belt through the buckle. He holds the loop open with one hand, keeping it open, keeping it big enough to fit over a man's head.

Green goes into the bathroom. It is steamy from the shower. Green pulls back the curtain. Aaron looks at Green, squinting against the water's spray.

"What the fuck are you—" he says. Then Green is on him. Green gets the belt loop around the neck. He yanks the belt's tail above Aaron's head. The noose tightens. Aaron loses his footing. He slides onto his back in the tub. His fingers claw at the belt. The belt bites deep into his neck. Green tries to keep the angle right. He sits on the toilet and leans back like a man waterskiing. He puts his feet on Aaron's shoulders. He yanks the belt toward the ceiling. He feels the man's skull uncork from his spine.

Green stands back up. He lifts Aaron. Green's body shakes with the strain. He gets the belt over his head. He ties Aaron's body to the shower curtain rod.

Green stages the scene. He remembers the times he helped clean up an auto-choke death. He re-creates scene details. He leaves the water running. He puts the laptop on the toilet lid. He opens up four tabs' worth of porn. He goes real dirty with the selections.

He plays what will come next in his mind. A maid will find the body. She will be bought or frightened. Everyone will know the drill. The mess will be cleaned up. They will hide the evidence of a jerk-off death. They will clean up evidence of the murder along with it. They will slap a cover-up over his cover-up. No one will look close enough to dig down two layers deep.

He calls Victor from the car.

"Cleanup on aisle seven," Green says. He hangs up before Victor can ask him what he means.

He goes home. He writes. It goes slow. He leaves nothing out but his name. He leaves nothing UNSAID. He copies and pastes it into an e-mail. He sends it to everyone he can. He wishes Sarah could read it. It is a press release. It is a moral fucking inventory.

LOVE AND OTHER WOUNDS

I love you.

I watch you bleed. I pull back your sweatshirt. I rip the bloody cloth with adrenaline Hulk-hands. I watch blood bubble from the bullet hole, frothy and too fast. The bullet caught you high and hard where the shoulder meets the neck. The bullet burst out the other side of you and smacked into the liquor store's wall. And now you are bleeding too fast to live. Too fast for us to fix here on this dirty kitchen floor. You need a hospital. I tell you we will get you there.

Rift says no hospital.

We came back to his place after the job went bad. In the yard out back, Rift's dog barks, the kind of sound that calls up caveman fears from the base of your brain. The dog growls. It whips drool chains around like a biker looking to beat ass.

Part pit bull, part cane corso. All killer. So is Rift. He paces. He rubs on an india ink neck tattoo. He counts bloodstained money. He says no hospital. He says with a bullet wound, doctors got to call the cops in. He says after the doctors sew you up, the cops will make you for the liquor store job in two seconds. He says you'll give up me and my faggot ass in two more. He says once the cops get to me, me and my faggot ass will flip on Rift faster than a Chinese gymnast. He says after that one clerk went for his piece and plugged you, Rift had to do them both. He painted the cigarette shelf and the boner-pill display with a fresh coat of brains and hair. He says the two cooling bodies turn the job into a capital case for all three of us. He says it's a death jolt for sure if we take you to the hospital with a gunshot wound. He says if you're bleeding out, you die to save me and him. Too bad so sad.

I love you.

You can't talk. You are past talking now. Your eyes, beautiful and fear-wide, beg me. I tell Rift you won't say anything to the cops. I tell him I know how strong you are. I tell him that you have to go to the hospital. I tell him that I'm taking you and he can kill me if he wants to stop me. I stand up. Rift picks his pistol up from next to the pile of bloody money.

Rift says he's done fucking around.

One bullet in the head of each the Koreans behind the counter means the Ruger still has four shots. Plenty enough for me and you. He points it at me. He says he's chopping up one corpse or two tonight, my choice. He says he'll use our meat to teach the dog to hunger for long pig. Says if I want to be with you so bad, we can mix together in his dog's ass. Behind him the dog scratches the glass door and shows me his teeth, the back of his throat. It bites the air as an appetizer. I know I can't let you die. I know there has to be a way out.

I love you.

I move past him to the glass door. The dog goes epileptic with blood lust. I open the door. Time does me a favor and slows down. I dodge dragon teeth. I get the dog by the collar. I unchain him. I barely control him. My grip won't last long. I tell Rift to get the car started. I tell him I'm taking you to the hospital. I tell him there won't be any cops called. Maybe animal control at worst. Because by the time we get to the hospital, there won't be any bullet wounds left. I aim the dog at you. At your shoulder. Rift gets it.

Rift says oh shit oh shit oh shit.

I set the dog on you. The dog bites down hard. You scream. Of course you do. He resets his bite and gives you a death shake. He grinds the muscle of your shoulder to hamburger. He chews the bullet wound away. When it's done I rip him off you and throw him back in the backyard. He smears pink drool against the glass as he scratches at the door. I don't care. I'm done with him. I lift you. You've never been so light. I tell Rift to get the car. We don't have much time. You're bleeding so much faster now. He runs to do it. He's scared of me now. He knows I can do anything. I know it too.

I love you.

LIKE RIDING A MOPED

. . . and now, the last bad thing about my fat: my fingers can't find the bullet holes. They must be there, because they brought me down and now there is sticky blood mixing with the sweat all over, but my clumsy hands can't find what kind of holes just got poked into my body. Are they just little puckers in the flesh? Or is it worse than that? Are scoops of me missing?

Somebody will write about this on the Internet. I bet they call the article "Fatty and Clyde" or something like that. Everyone will read it and chuckle. And everyone will look at me and see something else, which is what always happens. That's how Benny got to me when I should have known better. He looked right at me and he saw me.

Men sit next to me on the Metrolink and talk about women like I'm not even there. I'm just the thing taking up two seats when the train gets crowded. Everyone shifts their body away from me. Nobody points and laughs unless there's a kid. Then the mom can try to shush the little kid and maybe smile an apology and then look away, tell the kid it's not polite to stare. Honest, it's okay when the kid stares. At least it stops me from feeling invisible.

The others, the adults, they look and they just see other things. They look at me and their faces change, and I see my reflection in every little gesture and twitch. They look away and I look away.

So when Benny puts his tray across from mine at the Galleria food court, I don't believe him for a second. But he is so pretty, really, like Brad Pitt in *Thelma and Louise*. Later on I'll learn that he's from Springfield, down in the opposite corner of the state, same as Brad. And once he'll even try to tell me that they're cousins. Yeah, right, I'm sure Brad Pitt just has dozens of relatives who work for the St. Louis mob. What kind of cousin, I ask, like your mother's brother's son or what? And he says, no, I mean cousin cousin, like that means something.

But all that comes later. When Benny sits across from me I'm sitting in a corner of the food court with my fried rice and egg rolls, thinking about the store. I want to be a salesgirl. Mr. Nesbitt laughed when I told him, and said he didn't know what he'd do without me working the computers. The salesgirls, like Amanda who sits in the middle of the food court, don't know half what I do about carats and cut and clarity, but they look like the kind of woman you want to drape in diamonds. And now I'm replaying the conversation in my head, the way Mr. Nesbitt won't look at me while he laughs at the idea. And then there's Benny staring straight into my eyes and asking if this seat is taken.

He sits across from me talking and smiling. I'm trying not to stare at him. The napkin I put over my General Tso's chicken is turning orange from the grease it's drinking. As soon as this gorgeous hunk gets up and leaves, I'm going to dip my crab rangoon in the General Tso's sauce and suck out the cream cheese. But he doesn't leave, and after he tells one lame joke he winks at me. I wonder if the girls at Nesbitt's maybe hired this guy or something.

I've met chubby chasers, and this guy isn't one. Guys like that like to say something about my size right away, to try and make me feel comfortable. Oh God, like how they like a woman with some meat on her bones. Like maybe they're planning on cooking me up later.

He's not looking around the room while we talk, either. Most men, when they end up in a conversation with me in a bar or something, they're always looking around. Maybe they're looking for better options, but mostly, I think, it's because they're afraid someone might see them. A friend told me this joke once. I guess it's a joke men tell to each other:

Why's a fat girl like a moped?

They're a lot of fun to ride, but you wouldn't want your friends to see you on one.

Benny looks right in my eyes when he talks to me. His eyes are clear blue, and I don't see myself reflected in them at all.

He asks if I want to go see a movie after work. I never told him that I worked at the mall. I could have been shopping. This is something I don't think about until later. At the time I can hardly think at all. But later on, it will come back to me and make perfect sense.

Back at the store, Amanda corners me. Her skin is the color of Arizona dirt, and it's stretched so tight you can see three sides of her collarbones. She asks me who I was talking to. Just some guy. Pretty cute, she says back, the way you'd say it to a niece who had not yet admitted to liking boys. Whatever, I say, just like your niece would.

After work, I stop at Lion's Choice and pick up a few roast beef sandwiches and eat them while I drive, barely chewing at all. He's taking me to dinner, and I'll be damned if I'm going to the restaurant hungry. He's not really going to show up, I tell myself as I drive and swallow. There's no way. Maybe he's just into fat chicks, I tell myself. But that doesn't feel right.

Maybe he's hogging, I think. I read one time about guys who will set out to pick up the fattest thing they can find, and they all show up someplace and the guy with the biggest girl wins. Wins what, I don't know. Respect? I can see in my head a table full of women like me, all of us knowing what is going on and not a one of us doing a thing about it while the men get drunk and laugh at us. For the hundredth time I cancel the date in my head and then remind myself that I don't even have this guy's number. My fate, at least for the night, is sealed.

It takes me about three hours to get dressed, an hour of that in the shower, getting everything, shaving my legs, even that patch down by my ankle. I have to hold my breath to reach it. I'm lucky I don't break my neck. Choosing a dress takes longer. Black, of course. Black's slimming, you know. I put my makeup on using a mirror and trying not to look at myself. Then I eat a pint of Cherry Garcia standing over the sink, thinking he's not going to come and if he does then that might be even worse and that there's something wrong with him; there must be some-thing wrong, but even if there is I don't care because at least that kind of wrong will be something new. When the doorbell rings, I just about bite through the spoon.

* * *

We eat Italian on the Hill, and I get fettuccini with white sauce and laugh at his jokes, which aren't very funny. He tells me he works in contracting, and I ask him what that means, and he fumbles a bit. So we drink more, and I let myself get drunker than I should on a date, because if I don't I'm going to jump out of my skin. Which wouldn't be so bad, really.

After the dinner, after I refuse to have dessert, just say no, when he asks me if I want to go to his place, I say yes. I breathe in deep, trying to see if my nervous sweat has kicked up any of the smell, but I don't smell anything. The way Benny smokes, I'd be surprised if he can smell anything at all. We go to his place in the Central West End and it's done up in that way that looks tasteful but just means that you bought everything at the same store. And I'm looking around and he puts a hand on my shoulders and it's like someone set my insides on puree.

When we make love, he wants to leave the lights on, but I stand my ground. He shuts off the light. He almost glows in the dark.

When we lie in bed the light through his window throws my silhouette against the wall, hiding Benny's completely. He doesn't try to put his arm around me, thank God. He sits up against his headboard and smokes and talks. He lets the name Frank Priest slip, and anybody who reads the paper knows he's like the biggest mob boss in town, and another part of Benny becomes clear. Then he asks me what I do. I tell him I run a computer system at a store in the mall. He asks what kind of store and I tell him, jewelry, and he says, oh, really?

Two nights later he takes me to a bar, and the other women look at me with hateful eyes like maybe I'm holding Benny hostage. Benny gets up at one point to get us refills and some guy with gelled hair and an upturned collar comes by my table, the muscles in his face slack and his eyes shot. He's trying to talk to me but he's laughing too hard to do it. At another table behind him his friends are tamping down their giggles like children in church.

The guy never gets his line out. Maybe it was about a moped, I'll never know. Benny comes out of the dark and doubles the guy with a punch in the stomach. Then he gets both hands in the crisp bristles of the guy's hair and slams his head against our table, making my amaretto sour jump. The guy just drops after that. Benny holds his hand out to me, palm up, and says, m'lady. His hand has little specks of blood on it. I take it in my own and I walk out of that place feeling like I left two hundred pounds sitting on the bar.

That night, after we make love, I tell him I know what it is that he wants. And that it's okay.

Yeah? He asks me.

Yes, I tell him. Just tell me what your plan is, and let's work together to make it better.

It turns out that his plan needs a lot of work. Benny doesn't know much about jewelry stores, or even jewelry. So I tell him about the security room and its own special server, which I can access. I tell him about the loose stone set, and how they keep another box just like it full of cubic zirconium fakes.

He talks about us robbing it together, like Bonnie and Clyde. You could wear a mask, he tells me. And I just look at him. A mask? What kind of mask could I wear?

He wants to blow the safe. He's already got a bomb, he says. He shows it to me, how you just twist these wires onto those connectors and then push down the little plunger and boom! Never thought I'd learn how to set up a bomb. When I tell him that we won't need to blow anything up, that the best stuff sits out in the inventory room so people can look through it, he gets a look on his face like I just took away his lollipop. He spent a lot of money on the bomb, he says. Well, it doesn't go bad, does it? I ask. Just put it in the closet, and maybe we'll need it next time.

Over the next two weeks I lose ten pounds. In that number there's a future where diamond money can buy the gastric bypass, buy new clothes, the kind of clothes they put in the windows of the stores at the mall. There's a future where people could see me and Benny at a bar somewhere and not laugh or gape or guess I'm his sister. And we finally come to make a plan that I'm pretty sure will work. When we finally get it all set out and planned, Benny gets out a bottle of champagne and after a toast he pours some of the champagne on me and licks it off, and I don't push him away or wonder how I smell. I just look up at the ceiling and see that other life hanging there, so close I can almost taste it.

The morning of the robbery, we leave from Benny's place, each in our own car. Just before we pull out, I get back out and head back inside. Benny gives me a look like, what? I just point to my stomach and roll my eyes. Let him think I have last-minute jitters. It takes only a minute to do what I have to do. Then we're on course.

None of the salesgirls hanging around the display cases say hello. My card opens the door into the back of the store. I boot up the store server, then buzz the door to the inventory room. Jack, a sweet old guy with a gun on his ankle, lets me in. I boot up the security server, then wreck it with a few clicks of the mouse. I act confused and ask Jack to check a connection across the room. While he does that, I put a little red sticker on the top of the loose stone case, the one without the fakes in it. Jack comes back and tells me the wires are plugged tight, and I say, well, that probably makes it the motherboard. Let me make a call. I step outside of the inventory room and dial Benny's number. He doesn't answer, but he's not supposed to. He's coming from the food court where we first met. He should be here in the time it takes me to take five deep breaths.

He wears a wig and dark glasses, and he steps into the store with his silver pistol pointing right at Amanda's face. With his left hand he grabs her by the hair and yanks her across the counter. That's how skinny she is. And then he's pushing her to the back of the store and one of the other salesgirls starts screaming. Benny pushes past me without even looking and gets Amanda to open the back door and then just pulls open the inventory door, because I zapped the electric lock when I fried the server. A few seconds later the gunfire starts.

Maybe Jack went for his gun. I don't know. But there are two loud pops and Amanda screams and then Benny is back out, kicking Amanda in front of him, the loose stone case in one hand and the pistol in the other. Right in front of me Amanda falls down and Benny points the gun down and there's a bang and all sorts of stuff slops out of Amanda onto the floor. I would never have guessed she'd have so much inside her.

Then Benny looks up at me, and even though he's wearing glasses and a wig I can see him perfectly, and he sees me, like we're both naked in the daylight.

I turn so I don't have to watch the gun barrel rise, or Benny's face when he pulls the trigger. That's why the bullets hit me in the back.

If it had gone according to the plan that both of us knew was a lie, then Benny would have headed out the door next to the Foot

Locker across the way; ditched his wig, glasses, and coat in the hall; and put the loose stone case inside the big plastic Gap bag he had tucked inside his pants. He would have gotten in his car and driven to the motel just past Six Flags on I-44. After the police questioning finished, I was supposed to drive there myself.

But first, I would have stopped at his apartment and unhooked Benny's bomb from the front door, where I'd hooked it up just before we left. I would have put the bomb back into the closet and gotten ready for my new life. But I guess Benny will just have to find it himself. See, Benny never really had me fooled. But he did make me hope.

Damn him for that.

AD HOMINEM ATTACK,
OR I REFUTE IT THUS

Frank's thumb, the one with the lump, popped when he picked up his fork. The lump had scared him when it first rose up, enough to send him to the health clinic. The man at the doc-in-a-box called it a Bible cyst and asked if he did a lot of typing. When Frank said he did data entry, the doc had nodded and told him to pay it no mind. Said something about repetitive stress. Said something about workers' comp. That was when Frank had stopped listening. A man who got his typing certificate from JeffCo Prison doesn't take workers' comp for a cyst. He just thanks whoever that it wasn't carpal tunnel, not yet anyway.

"I can't believe you," the voice said behind him. He tried not to listen. But they talked too loud to ignore.

"Well, you're the one making indefensible arguments."

The booth behind Frank. College boys. They came across the park to the Dogtown Diner late at night for the cheap coffee. Same as Frank did. They came to read and smoke, same as him too. Frank drank coffee and read anything paperback, because in five dry years he still hadn't figured out how to sleep without booze. A different doc, one at JeffCo, had told him that he'd gone and rewired his brain over twenty years of juicing. That's just the way it was.

Repetitive stress.

"Get off it, Owen. How can you say it's not raining outside? You can see the rain hitting the window."

Owen was the one sitting right behind Frank. That made him the one smoking the sickly sweet clove cigarette.

"I don't know that's rain, and neither do you."

Frank hadn't noticed Owen when he sat down, but he'd gotten a pretty clear idea of what his face must look like. That slicked back hair and the scraggly beard, the old clothes that cost more than new clothes did, and a face smug as a freshly wiped asshole. Frank would put a ten-spot on it right now.

"Are you high?" the other guy asked. "I can see the rain hitting the window, just like you can."

"There are so many wrong things in that little sentence," Owen said. "First off, you can't know that what you see and what I see are the same. Alienation. It's only been, like, the most important theme of art for the last thirty years. You can't know if I see what you see."

"Can we just study?"

"Look, you just think it's raining because you've been taught the idea of rain—that when you see liquid fall from the sky that it is rain."

"Fuck the trig homework, huh?" the other one said, slamming shut a book. "All right, fine. I think it's rain because it's always fucking rain."

"But just because something has always happened in the past doesn't mean that it will happen again. Hume proved that in the eighteenth century."

Frank nodded at Debbie walking by with a coffeepot. She filled up his cup. He watched her walk away, saw the Band-Aids on the backs of her heels where her shoes rubbed her raw.

Repetitive stress.

"And another thing," Owen said. "Your whole concept of 'rain' . . . The word is a symbol. Once you've applied it to the drops of liquid that you insist are falling outside, you've replaced the real with the symbolic. It's your idea of the word that you're talking about, not the real thing that may or may not be happening."

"Then what's the point of you talking right now?"

"Ha-ha. Words still have a symbolic meaning that can never stand in for reality, which must be experienced through the senses . . . and of course the senses can't be trusted either. That's the realm of the imaginary, and that's not real either."

"So everything we know is just, what, a seven-layer bean dip of bullshit?"

"Exactly. Unreality piled on top of unreality!" Owen lit another clove. "Look, nothing is certain. Every experiment they've ever done on eyewitnesses and the like prove that our senses can't be trusted. The Heisenberg principle shows that even by observing something, we change it in a way that we'll never fully understand."

"Christ, Owen . . . it's raining outside."

"You don't know that." Owen's gesture shook the back of Frank's seat. "What are you doing in school, man? I mean, in high school they teach you Newton's laws, and then you get to college and you learn that Einstein and quantum mechanics have shown that Newton was wrong. Antiparticles move backward through time. We don't know anything about things people have been studying for thousands of years. And you look through a piece of glass and proclaim you know exactly what is happening out there. Don't be so stupid."

"Fine, Owen, fine. You win. It isn't raining outside."

"Fine, Jack, fine," Owen said. "Run away into sarcasm. But it's just because you can't prove me wrong."

For a second, just the sound of silverware scraping on plates. Frank rubbed the lump on his thumb, then the lump in his pocket, where the knife was.

"Look, dude, let's get back to trig."

"Pure mathematics, Jack. No problem."

Frank got up and paid at the counter, enjoying Debbie's twisted front tooth as she bit her bottom lip counting out change.

"Keep it," he said. "Slow night, huh?"

"It's the rain," Debbie said.

"I know."

Frank waited in the back of the gravel parking lot of the diner for the time it took him to smoke three cigarettes, looking into the diner at the two college students. Flicking his knife blade open and closed. He'd been right on the money about Owen. Only thing he'd missed were the thick-rimmed glasses.

Right about when Frank tossed the third butt onto the wet gravel the two young men closed their books and paid up. The one named Jack left the diner and headed south into Dogtown. Owen headed north, toward the bridge over the freeway into Forest Park. Frank followed.

Away from I-40, Forest Park was silent, and the trees above blocked out the moonlight. Here in the heart of the park at three in the morning, you could fool yourself into thinking you were in the middle of a real forest. Frank sped up, staying quiet, until he was close enough to touch Owen.

"Hey there," Frank said. Owen froze.

Frank kicked the back of Owen's knee. Owen skidded down ass-first onto the wet grass.

"Is it raining?" Frank asked. He straddled Owen, sitting on his stomach. "Tell me, Owen. Is it raining?"

"What are you doing?" Owen twisted back and forth under Frank. He slapped up at Frank with soft hands. Frank had the mount. Frank had him cold.

"The problem with you," Frank whispered in the dark, "is that for you nothing's ever really touched you. You don't have any scars."

He broke Owen's nose. He waited for the screaming to stop before he spoke again. "That's how it works out here, Owen. Action, reaction. Good old Newton.

"Can you trust your senses? Can you look at this," he said, flicking his knife open, "and trust that it is a knife? A real knife, a thing that cuts? And if you don't trust your eyes, will you trust your nerves?" He moved the knife under Owen's eyeball, the point just touching the lid under the arc of the orb.

"Is this real, Owen? Is it? Can you feel the rain on your face? Could I scoop out your eye? Does your life feel real?"

A beat passed.

"Is it raining, Owen?"

They sat together, one atop the other, on the wet grass.

"Yes."

Frank got off Owen. Owen stayed flat on his back, rain beading on his upturned face. Frank knew that Owen was feeling it, every drop as it landed and rolled on him.

"You were right about one thing tonight," Frank called back. "Sometimes, just being observed can change everything."

HEART CHECK

Shermer hits the Huntsville yard hard as teen love. He peels off the shirt to let the tats do the talking. Everyone on the big yard knows his jacket the moment he touches turf. Day one and he's famous. Wait, fuck famous. Henry Shermer is goddamn notorious. Hair-on-the-ceiling, brains-on-the-wall, evening-news notorious. Cons shoot side looks at him—no eyefucking allowed.

His skin is a textbook of white power numerology. A "14 WORDS" inked across his stomach, read as: we must secure the existence of our people and a future for white children. An "88" on his throat—88 equals HH equals Heil Hitler. Between his shoulder blades, "28" as in BH as in Blood and Honor. An Othala rune like a vertical Jesus-fish swimming on top of his heart. And Shermer knows he has heart—check the five blue lightning bolts on his shoulder. He got them done in county during the trial by a con who'd strung together a sweet home-made rig. Five bolts means five bodies laid low on an Aryan Steel greenlight.

He scans the yard, classifies and organizes. The yard is Mexi Heaven. The Texas Syndicate rules Huntsville. But Shermer isn't worried about their numbers. They're too busy beefing with California transplant Eme soldiers to bother a white man. Besides, the wetbacks have mucho splinter factions. Raza Unitas: they look clean and play dirty. Hermandad de Pistoleros Latinos: crazy as anybody, their faces inked with handgun tats.

Scan, scan. Crips hold down the weight benches; Bloods seem at peace in the background. Cocaine money keeps the Mau-Maus from going buck-wild at each other too much these days. They set-tripped on the streets but kept the peace inside.

Scan, scan. White men playing handball. But no go—AB tats on a back show them as Aryan Brotherhood: peckerwoods too fucked up on crank and the rep built by better men to be real soldiers. Perry Mashburn broke with the AB ten years ago, sick of setting up meth deals with wetbacks in the name of the white race. He formed Aryan Steel and they built a castle out of corpses. Browns, blacks, skin-traitors, even screws. Each shank-specked corpse another brick in the wall. Shermer needs that wall. He knows brother Steels are on the yard somewhere—scan, scan, scan.

One of the AB brothers cuts Shermer off in the yard. Two more stand behind him. The ABs scope Shermer out and he sees his jacket write itself on their faces—Shermer is goddamn notorious. Shermer killed on a greenlight from Perry Mash-burn himself—Shermer's name means massacre.

In his cell Shermer has his clippings from goddamn *Time* magazine. *Time* knew dick-all. Every white con in the world knows the real score: Zach Dixon got sprung out of Leavenworth owing the Steel money. He'd taken out a loan from Perry Mashburn while doing two years for possession. He'd moved the money outside somehow. Probably the same way he'd moved his meth in: riding the Hatchet Wound Highway under his sister's skirt on visiting day. Then when the Steel showed up looking for his vig he'd turned rat and moved to protective custody. He rode out the last six months of his bit in Snitch City, where Aryan Steel couldn't reach him. Perry Mashburn spread the word when Zach got sprung back into the world. The word was greenlight on the skin-traitor, full brotherhood for the trigger. The greenlight had a condition: leave no witnesses.

Shermer was two years on the outside after his first real bit for armed robbery. He was bone-tired of hauling rebar for shit money. Hauling rebar kept his jailhouse swoll on, and real pussy was better than prison-punk chokefucks every time—but life like a civilian bored his tits off. He'd met some Steel brothers on the inside. Even behind bars they'd had something. Call it honor. Call it brotherhood. Something you couldn't get from wage-slavery. Something Shermer never had in his life. Something Shermer decided he couldn't live without. He cashed his last paycheck and went hunting.

Shermer knew Zach from back in the day. He asked around and learned the lame bought heavy meth from local peckerwoods with the money he'd snuck out of the joint. Zach knew he couldn't stay still. He'd loaded up and gone on the run. Shermer followed. He tracked him down I-44 through Oklahoma. Missed him in Okmulgee. Got the story from a Waffle House waitress with a triple chin and death's-head earrings: every town he went, Zach made the scene at the white power rock shows. He followed Steeltoe H8 on tour, selling meth blasts at the show to pay his way.

Shermer stopped at a truck stop. Grabbed a coin-operated shower, a cheeseburger, and a computer kiosk. He checked the Steeltoe H8 website for coming gigs. He loaded up on black coffee and drove all night. He leapfrogged Zach at Tyler and set up camp in Houston—the local skinheads called it Space City and ate migas while cussing out wetbacks. Typical soft-shell motherfuckers. Shermer knew the warrior blood still flowed through their veins. But it was gone from their faces.

Shermer sat in the parking lot while Steeltoe played their set for a warehouse full of Hammerskins and peckerwoods. Shermer caught sight of Zach. He knew him from his butt-crack chin and his meth-rat eyes. He could have iced him in the parking lot before the show, but the greenlight said no witnesses. Shermer wanted full-tilt brotherhood or nothing at all. The Steel had to know he was a righteous warrior.

He followed Zach from the show to a motel on the edge of Space City. The dude had people inside the room. No witnesses. Fuck waiting. Shermer wasn't a bitch-made bushwhacker. There was more than one way to leave no witnesses. Shermer mounted up with a shotgun and a head full of Viking dreams. He came through the door with the twelve-gauge breakdown in his hands. Five seconds in, Zach looked like Picasso painted him—head over here, arms over there. Two more pumps wiped out his partners. Shermer breathed blood mist. Some little featherwood just picking up some crank made it halfway out the door; a buckshot rip left half of her in the room and the other half rolling down the sidewalk.

Four bodies, no regrets. He'd heard you felt things the first time. He didn't feel shit.

He found the featherwood's six-year-old son hiding behind the shower curtain. Sirens on the highway said hurry. A cop car nearby. Shermer's bad luck. The kid cried and cried while

Shermer reloaded. Perry said no witnesses.

If he was a nigger they would have gassed him for it.

Instead they sent him for a ride at Huntsville that would last as long as he did. Life with no parole. The old cons called it "all day." All day wasn't shit. And neither were these AB lames set to give him a dick-measuring right out in the yard. Shermer checked hands. No shanks—didn't mean shit. Convicts know how to hide, how to stash. Motherfuckers could have a god-damn samurai sword hidden somewhere—Shermer wouldn't see it until the word go.

Shermer weighed odds—best bet said these peckerwoods were straight-up heart-checking. A yard shank was plain stupid. Shanks don't have blades, shanks have points. No throat-cut, no slashes, just stab stab stab. Try to stab a man to death—it ain't easy. Can't slice open the arteries, can't dump guts onto the floor. Stab a man a hundred times and maybe he dies, maybe he doesn't. Doctors work miracles on septic shock and puncture wounds. Stab a man on the yard, pigs in the tower lay you out— and high-powered rifles do kill easy—and your man spends a month in the ward and walks out good as new.

"What's up?" The guy in front, billy goat pubes on his chin, drops the words. It's a greeting, a question, a challenge all in one. Shermer smiles—fuck your sister spelled out in teeth.

They don't swarm. They just want to see what kind of man he is. They're fucking lames. They're heart-checking Shermer.

So Shermer turns it back on them. He drops major eyefucks on them. He dares them to say boo. In a few seconds they're going to have to tangle just on general principle. Shermer saw plenty of yard stompings in his last bit. He knows he just has to hurt one of them bad and not stop fighting when the stomping starts.

"You kill a kid and still call yourself a white man?"

This shit here is why the Brotherhood ain't shit. This shit here is weak. Fucking lames. Fucking punks. Shermer can't say what needs to be said—a Perry Mashburn greenlight gets followed to the letter, and that's what makes us white men and you shit. Fuck the law, fuck life, fuck dead kids, fuck the whole motherfucking world. It is what it is. Shermer can't say it—the words would turn to warrior cries in his mouth. These lames wouldn't understand nohow.

Shermer gets ready to get down. His muscles don't move. It's all in the eyes.

"Hey, now."

The voice comes from behind the AB lames. Aryan Steel—the cavalry has swastika neck tattoos. Four brothers—Shermer counts quick—eleven blue bolts between them. The one in the lead—he's got a ring of shank scars on his torso like a shark bite. He's got a screaming eagle tat over his heart. He's got four blue bolts on his arm. He's got a name that rings out in every lockdown—Craig Hollington. In the cellblock legends they called him Crazy Craig. Shermer knows the stories. Crazy Craig pushed Blood Nation OG Goldie Webber off a third-floor walkway with a bedsheet noose around his neck—Crazy Craig brought lynching back to Huntsville. He got sprung from death row off some lawyer shit. He rules Huntsville for Perry Mashburn. He's the thick dick in this yard. A Real White Man. The man Shermer came here to meet.

"He's with us, y'all hear?" Crazy Craig talks direct to the one with the billy goat beard. Shermer makes sure to remember billy goat's face—he'll ask the Steel for details later.

"Fuck it, man, you guys stand up for a dude what kills—" Crazy Craig gets closer to the AB dudes.

"We take care of our own, dog. That's how we do."

The men stare at each other. The yard smells like burnt

rubber and sweat. It smells like that Space City motel room. Shermer wants to smash/stomp/kick/gouge. Shermer wants to get down.

The AB dudes step off. They moonwalk back to the hand-ball court. Shermer slaps hands with Aryan Steel. He meets Crazy Craig and Moonie and John-O and Dag. They compare tats. They walk over to the heavy bag—Aryan Steel's turf. The Steel gather around Shermer. They give him the scoop—long-term truce with the Brotherhood and most of the esses. A war simmers with the smokes—they still got a hate-on for Crazy Craig thanks to Goldie's swan dive.

"I know you ain't no fucking lame," Crazy Craig tells Shermer. "But we got to see what you got, y'all hear? Get on that bag. Let's see how you gonna take it to the jigs."

Moonie holds the heavy bag. Shermer wraps his hands with ribbons of cloth. He's got focus. He's a wicked street-fighting southpaw. He goes to work. Right-right-left-right-LEFT-right-right. And again.

Jab-jab-HOOK-jab-cross-HOOK-HOOK. Moonie lets the bag hang free. Shermer sets it swinging. Crazy Craig tells him to move his feet. The Texas sun drinks his sweat. His blood thumps in his head. He punches to its beat. Jab-jab-feint-cross-jab-SHOVEL HOOK. The bag hits back on the swing. Shermer's arms jelly up. He takes a step back to catch his breath.

"Get back in there, son."

Crazy Craig grins. Shermer reads it: They've seen he's got guns. Now they want to see if he's got heart. He steps back in low: HOOK. Sounds like a shotgun blast. The Steel whistles and hoots. Minutes pass. Jab-jab-HOOK. They want to see how far he can go.

Left-left-right-LEFT. His pulse so hard his eyeballs throb. Minutes stretch out. No one says stop. He shows the guys more.

Jab-jab-jab. He can barely get the arms up. Left-left-left. He trips on his feet. He goes down. He can't breathe fast enough.

The Steel picks him up. They clap his back. Yard time is over. They walk him down the halls. He still can't lift his arms. He still can't catch his breath. Colors come out of nowhere. His heart swells twice as big, and his rib cage feels its every twitch.

"Good job there, Sherm," Moonie tells him. In a crowded hallway. They stop. Moonie takes the wraps off Shermer's hands. Shermer's fingers can't close. They glow red with rushing blood under the skin. Moonie puts the wraps on himself. He looks at Crazy Craig. Craig nods. Moonie walks down the hall toward the brothers.

"What's—what's happening?" Shermer can barely get it out. His lungs feel rusted.

"Part two of your initiation, brother," Craig says. "You got your blood pumping?"

"Hell—hell, yes."

"Well, check this shit out."

Moonie walks into a crowd of Bloods and swings—a perfect punch, a tripod of feet, fist and skull. The Bloods step back—Moonie stomps—the blacks swarm him. Shermer understands. Moonie's a distraction. For whatever Shermer's next test is. His guess—they want to see him kill. They still got to see his heart. He tries to pick out the biggest smoke in the room for his victim. He hopes his battered hands can still handle a shank.

The guards swarm. They toss Moonie and his opponent to the floor. Before Shermer can see if Moonie is in one piece, Crazy Craig puts a hand on his shoulder, leads him down a hallway Shermer hadn't seen before. John-O and Dag are at his back. He can still hear the hacks screaming, trying to get control.

Shermer calls the distraction accomplished. Now it's his turn. Initiation.

"Y'all got heart, brother," Crazy Craig tells him. "You truly do. Perry Mashburn sends his regards." Shermer stands exhausted, triumphant. Ready for baptism in blood. Ready to be born again in brotherhood.

"But," Craig says, "he says you shoulda known better than to kill that kid."

Shermer sees John-O and Dag coming at him. Warrior instincts kick in. He grabs for them. Useless. A waste—they'd made sure Shermer had punched himself out. Shermer's mind churns. What are they thinking? He's goddamn notorious. He left no witnesses. He lived the code.

Crazy Craig brings out the shank—looks like a railroad spike. He sticks Shermer in the center of his Othala rune. Under the spike, his heart still beats crazy mad.

"Fuck you!" Shermer says.

"Some other day, some other dude, maybe fuck me. But today it's you."

Craig hammers down the shank with his palm. It splits Shermer's heart. He sees blood hit the ceiling. His brothers drop him to the floor and he sees nothing at all.

ALWAYS THIRSTY

Tommy dreamed of whiskey sweet as Southern tea. The dream had no sense of place or sound. Just a bottle at his lips and swallowing. Great gulps filled him with booze until he was liquid too. He drowned in himself.

He woke up gasping, a man breaking the surface of a lake after a deep dive. He found himself in his bedroom. The sort of thing that shouldn't be a surprise. The sunlight came in low. It pulled shadows across the room. Dusk or dawn? He looked at the alarm clock. Saw the red dot. Dusk. Shit. He had to get ready. He had to get . . .

Geat.

Tommy listened. Nothing but the sound of blood rushing hard and loud in his head. The last time Geat had come up to St. Louis and crashed on Tommy's couch, his snores had woken

Tommy up in the next room. But now nothing. Tommy got up slow. The ache of his hangover went deeper than bone. He checked the couch. Maybe the gods who took care of drunk fools had put Geat there in the night.

No.

The blood in his head got louder.

Tommy covered his face with his big hands. They stank. He dug them into the hollows of his eyes. Tried to blot out the world. He took in air and tried to piece together what parts of the night he could remember.

He'd met up with Geat at the Pickled Punk the night before. Geat, the finest watchdog in the Ozarks. The two men had worked together plenty over the years. Folk in the bar gave them a wide berth. Two great big sons of bitches radiating bad motherfucker.

They took a table in a dark corner. Tommy talked quiet as the jukebox let him. He walked Geat through the job.

Geat had done a little work for Lambert before. He didn't need much to get the picture. Lambert bought junk from the Bosnians in South St. Louis. He stepped on it and sold it to the black kingpins in North St. Louis. Good clean business. Tomorrow night was the re-up. Tomorrow night, Tommy and Geat would take a duffel bag full of money down to Little Bosnia and pick up a duffel bag of junk and drive it back to Lambert's no-name bar on Dirtnap Avenue.

"I never dealt with no Bosnians before," Geat said. "What're they like?"

"Same as anybody else," Tommy said. "They won't fuck you over, long as you don't give them a chance to do it."

Geat got it. He was a pro like Tommy. He knew a watchdog was like the man in the circus who worked with tigers. Everything goes fine, long as you never let them see you as a piece of meat.

They set to tearing the night down. One, two, three, four shots and a couple of beers. Nikki, the owner of the Punk, had laid one hell of a stinkeye on Tommy from behind the bar while she poured the last round of shots. But so what? She didn't have a say in his life. Not anymore.

They rode together in Tommy's truck to the Broadway Athletic Club. They watched kid boxers from folding chairs—the back row, close to the bar. Tommy switched to pale whiskey and Cokes. After the fights Tommy and Geat wandered onto the redbrick streets of Soulard. The night had rolled for them then. Like the world was fitted with ball bearings.

They'd wound up in some blues bar full of hoosiers. Tommy was getting numb. Started getting the itch. Nikki had been the one to name it in one of their fights near the end of it all. She called it the drunkard's paradox. Everybody's got their share of pain, even though it always feels like more than their share. Pain is part of the deal. Painlessness outside of death is an unnatural condition, she'd said. A man can't get to where he's feeling no pain for too long before it starts to itch at him. Before he starts to notice the hole where his pain's supposed to go. Pretty soon he starts needing the thing he was just running away from. Fiending for pain. That was Tommy, she said.

Geat made conversation with a table of men and women from South County. One of the women, a silver streak in her hair like Nikki's, leaned into her man and whispered something that made the man's eyes come alive with lust. Tommy, the itch burning now, told a joke. He told it loud, with fuck-you eyes for the whole table.

"How do you get a South County gal to suck your dick?" he asked. "Put ranch on it."

The South County boys, filled up with liquid courage, got riled up. Geat tried to squelch it. Him and Geat had been out-numbered five to two. Bad odds for the South County boys. Tommy got the taste of raw hamburger and copper wire in his mouth. The taste of blood. His body's way of saying shit was about to go down. Like how an old-timer's leg ached and he'd know rain was coming. The soberest of the South County boys had gotten a better look at Tommy and Geat—jailhouse tats, gorilla hands, bodies built for violence, and eyes that had seen plenty of it—and got his friends to sit the fuck down. Tommy had laughed about it and taken another shot.

And there it was. That shot had been the one that cut off his mind from his senses. What happened after that might as well have happened to another person. A lot of Tommy's life was like that.

He popped aspirin, stuck his face to the kitchen faucet to wash them down. He gulped water. His throat burned. His tonsils were stomach-juice fried. He must have puked sometime when he'd been floating pilotless. He smoked a stove-lit cigarette hard, like it had the cure in it. He checked the fridge for the last beer, the one he knew he'd already drunk.

Tommy's cell phone showed a dozen missed calls from Geat. He felt hangover panic like jolts of electricity through his chest. Tommy hit redial. A lump of cigarette scum sat heavy in his throat.

"Hey there, motherfucker." Geat's hillbilly twang got thicker when he was pissed. "A day late and a dollar short in the callback department."

"Look—"

"That was a hell of a way to leave a man hanging. After you

split on me," Geat said, "those South County boys got their mettle back. Five-on-one and all."

"I split on you?"

"Yeah, man. I went out lookin' for you and they followed. Shit, I had to break some son of a bitch's arm to get them off me. Still got stomped pretty good."

"Where you at?" Tommy asked. "We've got a job to do."

"Ain't you got some nerve," Geat said. "I'm back home now. I got the fuck out of St. Louis. Drunker'n hell, but I made it."

The silence was loud. Geat was the one who broke it.

"What happened to you, man? You used to be class."

He hung up. Tommy held the phone to his ear for a long second. Then he went looking for that phantom beer again.

The air felt hot and wet as dog's breath. Tommy kept the windows down. He drove downtown. Tried to sweat the poison out. Fought down the thing in his head that didn't want to think about the mess he'd put himself in. No Geat meant he'd blown the deal. It meant telling Lambert that he'd fucked up. Stomach acid brewed at the thought of it: Lambert with his eyes that never changed no matter what his face did. But Tommy had no choice. He had to come clean to Lambert, tell him he fucked up and needed another man.

His left arm ached. His fingertips soda-pop tingled. His breath drew hard. Classic heart-attack symptoms. Classic bullshit. His brain just gave him the signs of one sometimes on days like today. When he was half-poisoned with a fuckup hanging over him. When the real thing came he would most likely ignore it, thinking it was just his brain fucking with him again.

He turned onto Dirtnap Avenue. The street signs called it Napoleon Avenue. The street signs were wrong. This was Dirtnap. Redbrick skeletons and fizzled-out streetlights. Gang graffiti and broken windows. Don't walk in the alleys unless you like getting drunk-rolled. A sign written in Nikki's hand had been stapled to the door of the Pickled Punk: DO NOT PARK ON SIDE STREETS. YOUR CAR WILL BE STOLEN. The sidewalks sparkled with broken safety glass. The kids around here loved stolos—stolen cars boosted for the pure demon fun of it.

Tommy opened the door to the bar. The stench of spilled beers and cigarettes rushed out to meet him. Five red-topped barstools and an Old Style sign above the bar. The stickers of a thousand dead bands papered the walls. Tommy slid onto a barstool. Nikki worked the bar. She still looked good to Tommy. Wet eyes, slick with life and the brains behind them. Hair, black and shining with one gray streak, poured down past her shoulders. Tits just starting to sag—but just enough to make them feel real when you took them in your hands.

It'd been years since he'd been able to do that.

Tommy and Nikki had been all fireworks—Roman candles pointed at each other's faces. They had raged. Lived hard, drank hard, fucked hard, fought hard. He needed the fireworks for the heat they gave him. Everything else in his life felt cold. But things changed, the way they do. He drank more, drank alone more. They fought more, fucked less. She loaned him money when things got slow with Lambert. He never paid her back. Neither said the thing: his end of the seesaw went down, hers went up. The rest of it was white noise. So it ended. A few years passed. They found their truce as bartender and regular. Old friends. But never that other, better thing.

"Where's your friend?" she asked now. Thoughts of Geat brought acid up the back of his throat. Refried his tonsils. Made him thirsty.

"Vodka. Double." Odorless vodka. The secret drinker's best friend.

"At least say 'tonic' for me, Tommy."

"Sure. Tonic, why not?"

She gave him the drink. He pushed back a twenty. He made himself wait. She turned her back to him. Then he picked up the drink. He took it down fast. It ran cold-hot down his throat. Warm numbness spread. He opened his eyes to see her watching in the mirror behind the bar.

Lambert's place down the road from the Pickled Punk had been a bar once itself. The Black Goat. Brains and eggs specialty of the house. Now it wasn't really a bar. It was a lair. Still fully stocked with booze. Just missing customers.

Lambert and Meadows sat at the single table in the middle of the room. Tommy came in to the sound of their laughter. Meadows laughed with his whole body. Crooked-tooth grin. Lambert laughed every place but his eyes. Icebox cold. Nikki had joked that Lambert needed Meadows there to remind him of what humanity was like.

"Sorry, man," Meadows said as Tommy sat down, "but I got to tell you, you look about half dead."

"Just half dead?" Tommy said. "Guess I still have work to do." No laugh.

"Where's Geat?" Lambert asked.

"Running late," Tommy said. He hadn't planned on lying, he lied to himself. "He found himself a little something-something last night, and I guess he's putting her through the paces. I'm going to get him on the way to Little Bosnia."

Lambert just looked at him. Those fucking eyes. Like he fucking knew. But he didn't know.

"You know Geat," Tommy said. "He's a pro. We're all good."

"Need a piece?" Meadows asked.

"In the glove compartment." Another lie. His nine-millimeter sat in his sock drawer. He'd forgotten it. A stupid lie. Meadows would have a gun. Hell, if Tommy came clean now, Lambert would probably send Meadows with him. All he had to do was say it.

He didn't say a thing. He let the moment pass. Lambert pushed the duffel bag over to him. It was done. Tommy sipped the whiskey before he left. He didn't gulp.

Well, maybe a little at the end.

Tommy hit Little Bosnia. The cash rode shotgun. Storefront signs turned from English to symbol salad.

Tommy pulled into the lot behind the restaurant, pushing his huge truck between two tiny Japanese sports cars lowered until they would scrape speed bumps. He looked to the shotgun seat. The duffel bag where Geat ought to be. The gunless glove box. He thought about driving away. Seeing how far that bag of cash could get him.

But he knew the answer. Not far enough.

He got out of the car and walked into the restaurant.

Families everywhere. Children ran between tables. Mounds of ash heaped in the ashtrays. Bottles bumped into plates of sausages and fried things. Parents shouted at the children. They shouted at each other. They shouted at the air itself.

The bar sat in back. Men in cheap-looking black suits. Smoking, drinking. A man in a bright yellow suit behind the bar. He smoked two cigarettes at once. He had scars on his face from some batshit Eastern European madness from whatever the fuck went down back there. Tommy knew him as Balic. He was the Man in Little Bosnia.

The men in black suits eyed Tommy as he slid up to the bar.

Tommy held the duffel bag between his knees. Anyone making a move would have to come through him to get it.

"Hey," Tommy said.

Balic flashed brown teeth. A dog's threat as much as a grin.

"Hello, my friend!" he said, lifting a glass of blush liquor at Tommy. "Welcome."

"You know why I'm here."

"Yes," Balic said. "And you will wait."

"That's what you got to say, huh?"

Balic poured two shots of the blush liquor into highball glasses and pushed one toward Tommy. Tommy downed it and wiped his mouth. Some kind of fruit brandy. It burned like heavy fuel. Like one hundred proof. Balic waved at the crowd of families.

"You are early, is all. The merchandise is not yet here. We don't do business during business hours, you see? You will have a drink and wait."

The glass of liquor filled in front of Tommy. He drank it. The bottle sat next to his right hand. He poured himself another. Lit a cigarette. He felt that thirst. The one that grew the more he drank. He gave it what it wanted. Plenty. It tasted like burning fruit. Copper wire.

One by one the families left. The men smoked and talked. They told jokes. They started telling them in English for Tommy's sake. The jokes had two idiots in them, Mujo and Suljo.

One of the men knew how to tell a joke. He's got one for Tommy, he said. Mujo and Suljo are walking home to their village after a raid by the Serbs. They find a head by the side of the road. Mujo looks at it and says, I think this is our old friend Naser. No, can't be, says Suljo. Mujo picks up the head and shows it to Suljo. Look at it, he says, this is certainly our old friend Naser. Impossible, says Suljo. Why is it impossible, Mujo asks.

Suljo points at the head and says, Because Naser is much taller than that!

The men laughed. Tommy laughed. He leaned back. An arm wrapped around his throat. He had just enough time to wonder why they just didn't put a bullet through his brain. The arm around his throat squeezed. Nothingness bloomed at the edges of his eyes. He planted his feet against the bar. Pushed. The man choking him came down with him. They hit the floor. It seemed like Tommy should have felt something.

Tommy wrapped his hands around the duffel bag straps. The animal inside him said, Run. He tried to scramble to his feet. The men grabbed him. Hands from behind pulled him up. Balic put his face inches from Tommy's.

"I have a message to send to Lambert," he said. "Give me that bag and you can give the message with your mouth. Do not give it to me and I will write the message on you."

"Fuck you," Tommy said. It felt good to say. He rolled his shoulders. The men holding his arms struggled to keep hold. Balic hit him in the stomach. Tommy puked air. Dropped. He didn't feel anything. His lungs refused to start up again. Balic stomped his head. The world blinked out.

It blinked back in. Three men left in the room. Balic and two of the black suits. The two men in black held his arms to the ground. Balic grabbed a vodka bottle. Broke it on Tommy's forehead. Bloody vodka splashing down into his eyes. Little rivers plugged his nose. Balic stomped him. And again. Something cracked. Tommy didn't feel any of it.

Tommy turned his head and watched the blood pool below his face. Black and spreading. Hands turned his face back to the ceiling. Balic stood over him with a knife. He pushed the knife into Tommy's stomach. His body jittered. It knew it was being gutted. But Tommy didn't feel it. Vodka and blood and blackness and Tommy all mixed together, like he was the world and he was drowning in himself.

He gasped like breaking the surface of a lake. He roared. Balic stood over him, still working with the knife. The pain of it all rushed into him. He drove his boot into the fork of Balic's crotch. Balic dropped. He left the knife hilt-deep in Tommy.

Slick with blood. Tommy took a punch in the face from one of the men holding his arms. His head hit the floor. His teeth clicked through the tip of his tongue. His hands went to his stomach. Found the knife there. One of the black-suit men tried to wrestle him back down. Tommy stabbed strobe-light fast. Hit something major. Now the blood wasn't just his.

Tommy moved toward Balic. His feet went spastic. He caught himself on a barstool. He looked down. So much blood coming out of him. More black than red. Dark with life like soil.

The still-standing man in black tried scrambling over the bar to get away from Tommy. Tommy grabbed him by the ankle with his left hand. With the knife in the other, he opened the man's leg to the bone. The man screamed. Tommy laughed and yanked the man down to the floor with his friend.

Balic reached for his gun. Tommy got to him first. He laughed and lunged. Butted him with a bloody forehead. Balic went slack. Tommy turned Balic over onto his back. Tommy hung his face over Balic's so his blood dripped like rain.

"I've got your knife, friend," Tommy told him. "Let me give it back to you."

Tommy gave it back. And again. It had been a while since Tommy had done any work with a knife, but the way of it came back to him quick enough.

Things Tommy will never remember.

Tommy drives through gray mist, like fog had rolled in

from the Mississippi and buried the city. Blood soaking him everywhere, down to his sodden socks.

He walks through the door of the Black Goat holding a heavy wet load.

Tommy lies on the floor of the Black Goat. Blood trailing from the back door. Meadows turns him over. Meadows sees that the messy thing he held in his arms is his guts, slipping through the gash in his stomach. Meadows carries him to the Black Goat's unused kitchen. Lambert asks him questions about money. About Geat. Tommy laughs pink foam.

There is a man elbow-deep in Tommy. Some doctor Lambert owns. He works Tommy's intestines with both hands. Shoves them back inside Tommy, hard, like a man overloading a washing machine.

Tommy woke up to a pain he'd never known before. Meadows and Lambert stood in the kitchen of Lambert's place. The never-used kitchen of the Black Goat. He wore his stinking jeans and a black T-shirt. He had an IV in his arm. Someone had gotten him a pillow. Probably Meadows.

"Is Geat dead?" Lambert asked.

Tommy ground teeth. The pain swelled from rivers to an ocean in him. The pain felt bigger than he was.

"He wasn't with me. He's back home."

"I know," Lambert said. "I talked to Geat."

Meadows started to ask, "Then why—"

"To see if he'd lie to me again," Lambert said.

Tommy told them what he could. About leaving his gun. About the attack. He thought he'd feel better once he told the truth. That's how it was sometimes in stories. People unburdened themselves of all the lies and they felt clean and whole again. Tommy didn't feel that way. He felt like a man who had needed to vomit and now had a lap full of puke.

"The doctor left some pills," Meadows said. He held forward a couple of blue capsules. "For the pain."

"No thanks," he told Meadows.

"You've got to take something," Meadows said.

His death had been so near him in Little Bosnia that he could still smell its stink. It smelled like gasoline, like hydrogen peroxide, something clear and pure and overwhelming. He'd run toward nothingness every night for the last twenty years. But when he'd seen it staring back at him from the inside of his guts . . .

He needed the pain. He needed to know he could take it.

Tommy took the pills. Lambert watched him. Tommy popped the pills under his tongue and held them there. He felt the capsules go sticky under his tongue. He fake-gulped. Lambert turned away. Tommy spit the pills out. He slid them under his pillow.

"Just one thing I want to know," Lambert said. "If you wanted to die so goddamn bad, why the hell did you fight them?"

The pain had colors. Red at the crevice of the cut where the steel staples pulled his torn flesh together and forced it to knit. The pain that spread around his body was yellow-brown, the color of old banana or Balic's rotting tooth. The colors washed over him. He opened his eyes and the colors went away, but the pain did not.

That night. Three in the morning. A summer storm roared against the building. Tommy's moans came out of his throat like solid things. He tried to ride it out. He tried to take it all. He broke.

He pushed his hand under the pillow (and that motion set upon him a new wave of pain, oh Christ) for the painkillers he'd stuck there. He lifted his head (stomach muscles contracted, sweet Jesus). Searched under his pillow with a blind hand. The pills were gone. Maybe on the floor somewhere.

The bar in the next room. He could see the bottles through the wall with Superman eyes. Three rows of everything. Single-malt scotch with caramel color and the memory of oak. Smooth Irish whiskey. Corn-sweet bourbon, the city-slicker brother to rocket-fuel moonshine. Vodkas with frosted bottles and fancy names. Sweet toxic-green Midori and ghost-pale ouzo. Vermouth, on the rocks like Hemingway. Gin, juniper scented, medicinal. Cognac, with an amber glow and fumes that burned the eyes. Chase it all down with a beer: pale gold Budweiser, St. Louis original from the keg, Guinness, pop-top Old Style and Pabst, brown Anchor Steam. Pissy Corona cut with lime juice. He'd drunk them all, knew them, knew they could kill this.

A castle against it all, the agony and everything else. A mote of ice, towers of glasses. Drink until the booze filled him and blanked him and gushed out the gash in his stomach. Until he flooded himself.

He pushed himself off the table, the gash kicking up a silent scream when his feet hit the rubber kitchen mat.

Tommy walked with his useless eyes shut, fingers out front of him like a teevee sleepwalker until he made it into the main room.

A streetlight spilled through the windows. The red neon Red Stripe sign above the bar cast the clear bottles pink and the green ones black. Rain thudded on the window. An angry man wanting in.

He lifted the drawbridge of the bar and walked inside. A highball glass. And whiskey. He poured. The smell like gasoline vapor filled his nose. The whiskey would be sweet. Sweet as southern tea. And dark.

In the red neon light it looked like a glass of blood. He lifted it. Thought about Nikki. About running from pain and running back to it.

He threw the glass across the room. Shards flew. He fell on the floor. Something inside him exploded. He took the pain. He lay there and accepted his share of it. He lay there in sweat and tears. The pain didn't leave. Neither did he.

The rain pounded against the window and the blood pounded in his head. Tommy got up off the floor. The pain went through him and he took it. He walked out into the storm. It soaked him. Washed off the blood and the sweat and the stink. He stripped off his shirt. Ran a hand across his stapled stomach. Lived with the pain.

Down the street the neon lights of the Pickled Punk glowed. Tommy walked toward it. Laughed to think how Nikki would scream when he walked through the door. And then maybe would smile.

There was that question, the one Lambert had asked him. If he wanted death so bad, why'd he fight it so hard? And he had his answer now.

He still had to pay his tab.

YOUR FINEST MOMENT

Maybe you should kill her first, seeing as how she was the one who promised you true love forever and then went and sat on another man's dick. That is the first thing you think when you come back from a fishing trip early, drop by your girlfriend's place, and walk up to the apartment complex parking lot just in time to see her lead Danny Fucknuts in through her door. Your first thought is to take her and break her, jelly her face up with a rock, a tree root, something ancient and jagged. Smash her, crush her, make her slick and wet with blood.

You get drunk instead. You drink in a bar with a jukebox that some asshole has loaded up with country songs, old ones about lying cheating women. You start to doubt yourself. You wonder if you drove her to this. If you're to blame.

You take another shot and say fuck that shit. You ask for a

bill. You mention being a cop and the bartender rips up the bill. You give him two twenties for the half-full bottle of tequila and he gives it to you.

You wander through the streets near her place, where right then she is leaning back on her bed with Danny Fucknuts grunting over her. You think about barging in, about causing a scene, and something in you tells you not yet. You think about that portrait on the wall of her apartment. She made you pose for it at Sears two years ago, fresh out of the academy, fresh in love. You in your patrol uniform and her with her hair teased up to the sky. Your friends called you pussywhipped but you didn't care because it was true love. That photo of you is right now watching her bang Officer Danny Fucknuts. In your drunk haze you see yourself in that photo coming to life, breaking out of two dimensions, stepping out of the frame and strangling her right then and there.

You wake the next day floating in shit. You don't know who you are except a giant ball of drifting meat, poisoned and alone. Then it all smacks back into you and again you want her dead. But then you drink a little water. The iciness hits your stomach and spreads through your veins and you get cold and you get smart and you know, you fucking know, the first person the detectives would go to is you. They always suspect the boyfriend or the husband first. Who else could hate a woman that much but someone who let her crawl inside? Could be they'd look the other way. Could be they buy that blue brotherhood talk enough to let you slip by on a murder. It's happened before, maybe it would happen for you. But maybe not. And you can't risk it. You aren't some prick who is going to prison the rest of his life just because he fell in love. No sir.

But that doesn't mean that you are going to let this one ride. Somebody has to die. And you aren't a suicide. You are strong.

You might have sliced off your dignity for that high-test bitch, but you still have a stub left. And so here you are standing over Danny, watching him sleep, standing here so you can kill him. But kill him smart. Ice-water cold, my man. You have done it all cold as hell.

You run through the checklist. Your head is shaved bald, not too radical a hairstyle change from your everyday cop flattop. You aren't going to leave any hairs lying around. T-shirt, jeans, underwear, bought from JC Penney's today, paid for with cash money, straight out of plastic that evening, no chance to pick up secondary fiber evidence. No fake alibi. That's just another lie to get caught in. You haven't gone elaborate with the planning. Plans are threads for the homicide boys to grab.

You parked your car on an empty side street and walked here through the night, passing no commercial buildings with their security cameras. You've come at three in the morning, after the last of the last-call drunks are asleep but before even the shittiest-job-holding sad bastards' alarm clocks ring. You walked. You didn't sneak or creep. You walked up to Danny's place and walked in the garage. Danny has that cop certainty that no one will rip him off. Danny's little plywood door in the garage, the only thing he saw fit to put between himself and God's cruel universe, between him and the man whose woman he is porking, that door you opened up with a goddamn credit card.

You know Danny is alone, because you said good night to her a few hours earlier, and you drove past her house on the way here and saw her car. Danny hadn't gone to sleep without a load on in maybe a decade. He won't wake up unless a gun goes off next to his head. Funny, that happens to be the plan. But you don't think Danny will wake up with 145 grains of lead parting his hair and his frontal lobe.

The gun is the genius stroke right there in your hand. It belongs to Danny. Your backup piece is strapped to your ankle, but you don't see any reason to chance it when here is Danny's own pistol. Not his department-issue, but that World War II .45 he keeps in that box by the teevee. You can drop the gun right here next to him like you're a movie mafioso. Let them run every ballistics test in the world. Won't prove a thing. A perfect murder to leave the boys in homicide scratching their heads till their scalps bleed. And leave the bitch wondering. You smile when you think about how she'll lay awake and wonder . . .

You pull the trigger. The gun explodes in your hand, blowing off your trigger finger and the first joint of your thumb. The stumps sizzle and bleed as you drop the mangled piece of metal.

That bitch, that bitch, look what she made you do.

Past the weird darklights of the flash you see Danny sit up wild-eyed, floating in silence and gun smoke. With barely time to curse Fucknuts for taking shit care of his piece, you jump on top of him. With the first punch your half-gone hand screams out pain, but you hit Danny again. Crunch crunch. You grab the bedside lamp, both hands to keep the grasp, and you bring that lamp down with a thud and a pop as the fuckwad's skull breaks and then everything is quiet but your own stuttering breath.

Back comes the ice water and even in the dark you can see what you've done. Your perfect crime has devolved to shit. Chock-full-of-DNA blood is everywhere. Mixed together, you and Danny, just like you're both mixed up inside her.

The pain of your hand is once removed, like some other guy is telling you about it. That is just adrenaline keeping you in the fight, but you can't let it run the game. There is still time to make this smart. Not perfect, but smart.

First, off comes that pristine JC Penney's T-shirt to wrap your hand up. Your belt cinches tight to slow the bleeding. You have two choices. You can dump the body, but that is a fool's fucking errand. Stick the body into your trunk, leaving DNA everywhere. And then hide the body where? Bodies get found, and that is a truth that you know for sure. So that leaves option two.

Fire. You find a gas can in the garage. You turn on the gas jets in the kitchen to fill the house. The kitchen isn't far from the bedroom and the gas fumes will hit the flames and foomp goes the house, every little scrap of DNA sizzled like bacon.

You hear the car before you see the lights. The blue and red cherries light up the room like a disco, flash flash flash. The gunshot led to someone calling the cops. Didn't they know one was there already? You peek out the window, thinking maybe you shouldn't have turned the gas on so soon. Tendrils of the invisible stink sting your nostrils. Frank Robinson—you know him a little, talked to him over third-shift coffee and cop-bar beers—has parked his squad car in the driveway and is walking up the drive. Frank rides his squad car solo except for Bruno the German shepherd locked safe in the backseat. So you have only one cop to kill. One more, that is.

You pull your backup piece from your ankle holster left-handed and put it to the wall just to the right of the door where a good smart cop like Frank or you would stand when knocking on the door of a dark house. You wait one long second. Then comes the knock and you pull the trigger. And the whole world catches fire.

The clouds of gas filling the house catch spark from the gun, and the air itself blazes alive with fire for less than a second. You come out the other side of the flame cloud smelling the stench of your own burning hair. But it worked. You can hear the steady rage of flames on Danny's bed chewing up all that DNA. Too bad about Frank. He lies on the other side of the wall dying out loud. You look out the window past Frankie's body to see the car door open and some rookie shitfuck climb out and take cover on the other side of the Charger, barking into the radio. Looks like Frankie has gotten himself a new partner after all.

The house burns faster. You can go out the back and try to make it home and try to explain away the missing fingers and burns, but you know it is way past that. You've been fucked from the start of this, trying to play it cool and rational when it was simple and savage. You should have cracked her skull the way you were built to do. It isn't too late. Maybe too late to do it perfect. Too late to do it smart. But not too late to do it right. You come out the front door with a caveman yell and pop a few shots to keep the rookie down as you run past.

You hear the rookie let slip the dog, but you're full of animal joy and keep right on running. Heading toward her. You run fast and free toward your fate. It is your finest moment.

The dog takes you down in the street. Your front teeth shatter on the asphalt. Bruno tears out a tendon as you struggle to flop onto your back. You fire the gun into the air. You shoot down the moon. There are arms around you. You scream with a broken mouth.

That bith!

That bith!

That bith!

JOHNNY CASH IS DEAD

I drove all the way across town to cut up this son of a bitch, but it's these three flights of stairs that got me worried. Usually when a man goes to see another man on business, it's the other fellow that he needs to be worried about. But my leg was my problem. My left knee started stinging something fierce while I was coming from old North Springfield to the southeast where they built all the malls and new apartments. Some old folks just like to complain for being left alive so long. I'm not like that, but my knee is. I smashed it thirty years ago at Marion, wrestling with a convict and taking a tumble down some steps. It never liked walking up long stairs since.

In the Ozarks we get about two weeks of spring before it gets hotter than a whore in church, and this was one of those fine April days after the cold and before the thunder and the heat. A fine day for bad business. The whippoorwills were still singing when I got to that big apartment building on the corner of Glenstone and Cherry, and there wasn't any stirring in any of the apartments I could see. The building was cheap yellow siding with concrete decks for each apartment. Most of the decks had little black grills and a few beer bottles on them. Mostly young folks from the school lived there, and not many that age see the sun rise unless they didn't sleep at all.

There was a tiny red sports car, just like Mandy told the police, parked across two spots. And above it sat three stories' worth of concrete steps to the door of his apartment, number 309, just like it said in the arrest report I had there in the truck. There was a good chance I'd be using both hands on the railing before I made it to the top, and out in the open where I could look like an old man in front of God and the world. I parked the truck next to his car, cutting "Don't Take Your Guns to Town" off in the middle. My grandson tells me that folks his age are listening to Johnny Cash, but he's just a man in a costume to them. They can't feel the music in the aches in their bones. He's dead now besides.

I pushed the .38 into my pocket so I wouldn't have to hunt for it, made sure that the rope was in the bag, along with the knife and stone, the gauze, and the papers I'd taken from the courthouse. I reckon that was stealing, taking those files, but the court already decided that they'd done all they'd cared to with them. One of the papers was paper-clipped to the photo of Mandy, her eye blood-clotted, that they'd taken at the hospital. I shut the bag.

The climb burned hellfire on my knee, and my lungs started to feel like they were coated in molasses. Lucky not to have keeled over on the landing between floors, I leaned over against the wall a spell. I thought Louise would curse me for a fool for climbing them at all. I knew damn well she'd call me a lot worse than "fool" if she learned what I had planned for the rest of the morning. So I pushed her from my mind, got up that last flight of steps, and knocked on number 309.

It took a few times before I heard some rustling from the other side of the door. Heath Jackson opened it, looking all gummed up in the face and confused, wearing nothing but a pair of drawers. In court, he'd been spit shined and in a suit, but standing there in that doorway he looked gruff and dumb just like the sorry bastard he was.

I guess he didn't get too many old men with guts hanging over their belts and faces full of sweat coming to see him. He just stared at me without a hello or nothing. And he didn't see the gun until it was right there in his face.

"Son," I said, "you and I have a little business to take care of."

When I walked the turn at Marion, I fought a lot of convicts bigger and meaner than Jackson, and I'd always gone man to man. I figured that although it might feel easier to clout the man with my club, he might figure the next day he could whup me in a fair fight. I finished that idea before they even got it. You get the best of a man because you had a piece of iron and he didn't, well, you didn't best him at all. The fellow who shot Jesse James proved that. So it pained me to have to use the gun to get Jackson's attention. It was all bluff anyway. I had the drop on him, but the .38 wasn't cocked and there weren't but two feet between us. That young fellow could have snatched that gun from me right quick before I could have pulled the trigger and spoiled my day.

He was a big son of a bitch, too. He played ball in school, and had those fancy-cut muscles the young men have these days. They look real nice, but to me they're like flowers grown in a hothouse that would die if you planted them out in the real world. In my time I knew some farm boys who baled hay all day long, and maybe you couldn't pick out every muscle they had but you'd sure as hell know they were there if that fellow pasted you.

Like I figured, he couldn't make a move. It don't look like much from the side, but a barrel can look awful deep when you look straight down it. It grabs your attention. So I pushed my way inside, brushed right past him, and shut the door.

His place smelled like an old barroom. Empty beer cans with bits of ash around the hole were piled next to the phone on the counter that separated the kitchen from the rest of the room. That was where the sink was, and a garbage disposal, and I was going to be needing that later. The bigger part of the room had a couch facing a teevee four times the size of the one I have, and a small little dining room table with two chairs, which was just what I needed.

"Now you just have a seat and mind your manners and I won't paint the walls with you," I said.

He might have been half asleep when I got there, but he sure was awake now.

"What is . . . who are you?"

"Don't remember me? Well, a man sitting in the dock has other things to do besides look for old men sitting in the stands, so I don't take offense. I'm John Hendrix. Mandy Pearson is my granddaughter."

Every day he was in court, I was there. Just watching him talk with his lawyers. Looking all smug and serious and innocent as the judges and lawyers read motions and whispered at the bench. I sat there every day because Mandy needed representing, and her mother was barely able to make it through the day and her father is worthless and lives in another state now besides. I was there until the very last day. Charges just thrown out the window because Mandy took a shower to wash the stink of his touch off her before she got the nerve to call the police. "He said, she said," they said, and that was all they were going to do about it. I saw Jackson's cute little mask come off when the judge rapped the gavel. I saw that smile bloom on his face like a flower growing on cow shit. And I saw that prosecutor not look me in the eyes as he walked out of the room, and that was when I knew that if someone was going to stand up for Mandy, then it was going to be me.

"Now, sir, I think we'd better talk about this."

"Oh, we're going to talk about it all right," I said, "but you're going to sit down now or you'll be laying down in a second. Now take that seat."

The chair looked maple but wasn't as strong. But it didn't feel like he could bust it, either. So I got him sat down and had him put his hands behind his back and got the rope out. The whole time he was still talking a blue streak, but I didn't pay no mind. I worked the rope through the slats of the chair and around his wrists. I had him lace his fingers together behind his back so his thumbs were pointing up in the air and got to work tying the knot. My fingers aren't so nimble as they were, but I got it as tight as I could. I gave my hands a shake to get the sting out, picked up the pistol, and pulled another chair so I was facing Jackson from about six feet away, close enough to hear him good but far enough away to get a shot off if I had to. He was still talking.

" . . . and I want you to know the truth. I mean, don't you think you should hear the truth first?"

"All right, son," I said. "Let's hear your piece."

I can't remember all of what he said, but you should have heard it. A preacher caught in his neighbor's bed couldn't have talked any faster. He was wearing that mask again, but I saw where it didn't fit him around the eyes. Those were just cold; they didn't move or change with the rest of his face. You spend enough time around convicts and criminals, you learn these things. It's the eyes every time. He thought he was going to sweet-talk this hillbilly old man and he slipped on that mask like it was nothing. You might think it's brave to be able to smile at a man who's got you tied up and covered cold, but it wasn't, not this time. Even though I had the drop on him, he'd taken a look at my old jeans pulled up past my belly and my work shirt older than he was and didn't see a man like him staring back. He was just saying "good dog" to a bad one.

I opened up the bag at my feet and took the whetstone out.

"Maybe you think that you can try and tell me things are different now than they used to be," I said, "but I lived back then and I live right now and I'm the one who knows both. So let me tell you, there's always been fellows like you who think they're slicker than owl shit. Folks always wanted to get a piece of action before they were married, and quite a few always have. There's always been whiskey and beer and girls who like to try it as much as a man does. And there's always been bastards like you who think that's the easy way to get in a woman's drawers. I saw Mandy that morning. I saw her face, goddamn you."

"Now, wait a minute!"

"Be quiet now. I know that Mandy's telling the truth and you ain't. But even if I wasn't sure, it wouldn't matter to me. She's my blood and under my care, and you're not."

With that I pulled out the knife, long with an elkhorn handle and hard iron blade. That got him sitting up.

"What are you doing?" he asked.

I liked to hear the fear that he couldn't keep under control anymore. I scraped the knife against the grain of the whetstone, real slow, just for show. The blade was already sharp enough to split a hair, but I liked watching the scraping sound run up and down his spine with each pass.

"Well, now, I thought a long time about what to do with you. First thought was just to blow your goddamn head off, and it's not much more than you deserve. Not much more, but more just the same. So, like I told you, you just sit still and take what's coming to you and you'll wake up tomorrow.

"So I thought about cutting your pecker off to make sure you can't ever do again what you did to my Mandy. And I like the sound of that."

I let him stew on that for a second.

"But it wasn't your meat alone that did what you did. It was your hands that held her down and let you get your way. So that's how I decided I'd make sure you'd never hold another woman by the throat again. I'm going to take off your thumbs."

The chair proved itself right then; it didn't break. Jackson was breathing hard and high now, and his mask was gone and he looked cold and crazy at the same time.

"That's insane," he said.

"Did I say how I used to be a prison guard?" I asked him. A second full of nothing passed, so I went on. "Back in 1959, I was still pretty green, I drew the short straw for some serious overtime, driving a convict to Kansas so that he could be hanged. That's a long road, taking a man to die. Jimmy Carson and I drove Convict Rodriguez for six hours and he never said a word to either of us but 'please' and 'thank you.' He'd killed his wife and the man she was in bed with, so many shotgun shells that they were more puddles than people when he was done. And they were going to hang him for it. He knew he had to answer for what he did, so he didn't hold it against us for doing what we had to do. And my whole life I've thought more of that hanged son of a bitch than a lot of people who never did wrong, but never did right, either."

While he chewed on that I turned my back to him and cocked the pistol. I didn't want him to see I needed two hands to do it. Then I went to the phone on the counter and dialed three numbers.

"Nine-one-one emergency services. What's the nature of your emergency?"

"Miss, my name is John Hendrix. You need to send an ambulance and a squad car over to 1526 Glen Avenue, apartment number three-oh-nine."

"Sir, what is the emergency?"

"Well, there's going to be one bleeding man here in a few minutes. I'll try to sop it up, but you better send that ambulance quick. The squad car will be for me. Tell 'em I won't kick when they come."

"Sir—"

"I'm John Hendrix."

I heard the noise behind me and just got the gun in my hand before Jackson hit me from behind. My knee gave out with a pop I could feel inside my head and we were down on the ground, me on my stomach and Jackson on my back. My arm was trapped under my chest, the pistol in my face and gun oil in my nose.

Damn old fingers too rotten and sore to tie a goddamn knot the right way, that was what did me in. Jackson had gotten himself untied while I was talking, and now he was breathing in my ear as loud as a lover. His left arm wrapped around my windpipe and squeezed. And I didn't see my whole life like they say you do. No, all I saw was what Louise was doing right at that moment, sitting on the porch with a cup of coffee wondering where I'd gotten myself off to. Right then I wished hard that I could be pulling into the driveway with a bit of breakfast for her. But there wasn't any time left to feel sorry for myself.

I got my head lifted up the floor until the back of my head touched Jackson's cheek. That just made it easier for him to choke me and he squeezed and whooped. But it gave me enough room to lift the pistol off the ground. I had to twist my wrist as hard as I could and my fingers were shaking with the strain but I got the end of the .38 between my teeth. One hard push and the barrel scraped the roof of my mouth until the angle felt right. I pulled the trigger.

The bullet blew out the back of my head and smacked right into Jackson's face. He fell on top of me and we both bled out together on his living room floor. Which is good enough, I guess.

ACKNOWLEDGMENTS

Thanks to all who helped me shape these stories, and the editors and publishers who gave them their first homes. In particular, thanks to Todd Robinson, an early champion of these stories as a writing-group partner, editor, publisher, and friend. Read *Thuglit*.

Thanks to Nat Sobel, who waited for seven years while I got my act together.

Thanks to Megan Lynch for taking a chance.

Thanks to the writers who have made my time in television feel like a paid M.F.A., in particular Bruno Heller and Tom Szentgyorgyi.

Thanks to Elizabeth, who doesn't mind living in a world where everything talks.

ABOUT THE AUTHOR

JORDAN HARPER was born and educated in Missouri. He has been a music journalist, film critic, and TV writer. He is currently a writer-producer for *Gotham*. He lives in Los Angeles with his wife, Elizabeth.